The Smut Book

by

Tito Perdue

Books by Tito Perdue

Lee (1991)
The New Austerities (1994)
Opportunities in Alabama Agriculture (1994)
The Sweet-Scented Manuscript (2004)
Fields of Asphodel (2007)
The Node (2011)
Morning Crafts (2013)
Reuben (2014)
The Builder: William's House I (2016)
The Churl: William's House II (2016)
The Engineer: William's House III (2016)
The Bachelor: William's House IV (2016)
Cynosura (2017)
Philip (2017)
Though We Be Dead, Yet Our Day Will Come (2018)
The Bent Pyramid (2018)
The Philatelist (2018)

The Smut Book

by

Tito Perdue

Standard American Publishing Company-
Brent, Alabama
2020

CONTENTS

One

He still remembered some of the things that had happened in days gone by—dark moments growing forever smaller in the backwash of time.

And the weather—he could remember when it rained all night and then gave way to sunshine just in time. Glancing skyward, he perceived a muster of calico clouds probing the harbors of the sky. And that one of the neighborhood women had left off sweeping her porch and was watching him with concern. Turning in that direction, Lee bowed sweepingly and then picked up traveling northwardly again while avoiding the cracks in the sidewalk, a project made more difficult by the very numerous leaves that in recent days had begun to fall. He hummed. He was carrying a pencil box, two books bound together with a strap, and a pineapple sandwich in a brown paper bag. His clothes, too, were characteristic of him, save that today's shirt, which had come down to him from his cousin, wasn't something he would have chosen.

He halted at the intersection, and, while waiting on the traffic, scanned the row of houses that extended from block to block, even unto perpetuity as it seemed. Somewhere down there, there where the buildings became indistinct, that was where Cherise dwelled, a blonde-headed girl who had been accompanying Lee from grade to grade since the beginning of things. Had she already moved past this point on her trek to school, or should he tarry here in case she hadn't?

Each block had seven houses, each house had a woman sweeping off her porch, the morning news on the radio, and a yard jockey to which in old days one could have tethered his horse. Moving straight forward, he crossed over into a district of three-story homes, dark ones containing stained-glass lampshades and, often as not, a retired gentleman reading the newspaper in an armchair.

No doubt it was the comfortableness of these places, the high ceilings and gilded portraits on the wall, that had first inspired in Lee the wish to be retired also. Truth was, he did not understand why he wasn't retired already, why he had to walk to school instead of willing himself there, or how time itself could be as slow as it was and last so long.

Cherise never came, and Lee was reduced to waving back in a more or less friendly fashion to Preston, dashing past on his bicycle. Suddenly Lee stopped, disturbed to have noticed a quart of milk still waiting on Mrs. Jenson's porch, where it was bound to lose its flavor. He sought for her newspaper, relieved to find that *it*, at least, had been fetched inside. But he knew better than to gather up the milk and put it away in the woman's refrigerator, only then to end up being punished for it.

By this time, he had left the three-story homes behind and was migrating through a poorer sort of district where the economy had fallen into ruins. Eyes straight forward, he gathered speed, preferring not to look at the overflowing garbage cans, disabled vehicles, and the dogs who proved more and more militant as the homes they defended declined in worth. He knew a good deal about this area and some of the things that went on here. A house was losing its paint and was missing several of its roof tiles, deficiencies that his own father would have mended before they had taken place. A dead cat lay in the gutter—he did not understand these people—its belly broken open. Glad was he that Cherise didn't have to see it.

Soon he would have arrived at school and still have time left over to confer with Cecil and the others. That was when it came to him that he had left his pencil box at home, or even perhaps had lost it. Dizzied by it, he checked his pocket and hands. His money, however, was intact, as he testified by drawing out the coins one by one and counting each in turn. His health was satisfactory, and he had completed his homework in good fashion, as also Cecil's. And if he weighed on average about fifteen pounds less than the greater number of his acquaintances, yet was he also about eighteen months younger than the greater part of them by far.

Two

Conditions improved as he drew near to school. The Catholic church came up, out front the unforgettable sign of a bleeding heart encased in barbed wire. Moving on tiptoes, he progressed up to where the first of the shops began to appear among the homes—a florist, music store, and a narrow place vending cigarettes and magazines. Two blocks ahead, he could view the movie theatre, dormant at this time of day. He had expected, wrongly, that *Green Dolphin Street* might have exhausted its run by now. Just then two *girls* went by on bicycles, neither of them giving heed to Lee. Far away he heard a whistle shrilling, calling men to work. Autumn was even more advanced in the countryside, evidenced by the smell of far-away pumpkins rotting, neglected, on the stem. A dog, lost and mournful, beckoned from the hills that lapped the town. Lee harkened to it, waiting in the shade of a maple dropping leaves as big as manuscript paper, and just as crisp. The bees were lazy, and the last of the honeysuckle was throwing off the season's final spores.

It wasn't as if Lee had any grudge against *Green Dolphin Street*, but rather only that he had been promised *King Solomon's Mines*, scheduled for this week. However, it had always been like this, and he should have understood by now that for him it were best to expect *nothing whatsoever* from life. Thinking of it, he put on a dead expression and began to walk somewhat robotically toward the half-acre field where some hundred students had broken into groups and were whispering among themselves.

Right away he found Cherise waiting in the shadow of the
building, together with the plain-looking girl who chaper-
oned her everywhere. Indeed, as he thought about it, he
realized that both of the beautiful girls formed an island of
her own, each of them supported by two or three others
wanting to share in the glow. His eye, Lee's, traveled from
Cherise to Barbara and her followers, and thence to the
water fountain where Linda wore a bright red jacket, together with an analogous ribbon in her hair. The very last
he had expected was for the girl to notice him and then
throw up her hand and wave back cheerfully in spite of
their troubled history with each other. Her smile was
transfixing—he couldn't endure it—and made her more
beautiful still. He was even thinking of going and joining
her, which is to say until he was preempted by one of the
most contemptible of boys, a rangy person with chafed
elbows and the beginnings of a nasty little moustache.
This comported with Lee's usual luck, however, and he
could find no one to blame for it except the boy.

"You get that math done?"

Lee jumped back, startled and flattered that Cecil had
come up quietly and was standing just behind him. His
papers, Lee's, were confused; even so he soon identified
the two-page assignment that he had tried to render in
Cecil's primitive handwriting.

"Now you didn't go and get all of 'em right, did you?"

"Naw, I put a couple of errors in there."

Satisfied, the boy looked them over, folded the pages,
and stashed them away in the vest pocket of his leathern
jacket. He was dressed in boots, jeans, and a bright yellow
shirt open at the collar. He was five feet and seven inches
tall, his hair was the color of sand, and he weighed one
hundred forty-five pounds. He had powerful teeth, perfectly formed, that looked like kernels of white corn. With
but few possible exceptions, Lee doubted there was anyone in the entire system who could have stood up to him

in a race or fight or in automobile mechanics. Having du-
plicated the second and third grades, he was some two
years older than Lee, and possibly more.

"Want a cig?" (The boy offered him one.)

"Naw. Maybe later."

He didn't want, Lee, smoke in his eyes, not with so
many girls standing about. Within the past half-minute,
he had identified Sonya Hunter standing among her usual
circle, all of them talking at the same time. Had they seen
him conferring with Cecil? He waved to Darlene and then,
putting on a bored expression, shifted his gaze to a ninth-
grade girl in lipstick. Already nervous, he grew even more
so when, for one brief moment, he thought she might be
looking back at him. No, actually it was Cecil she was
watching, as he should have known.

"She's looking."

"That's okay, I don't charge for that."

She was still looking!

"Do you think I might grow up," Lee started to ask,
"and be somewhat like you?" "I think she wants you to go
over there," he said in fact.

"Let her come over here, she wants to. What, she got a
broke leg or something?"

No, Leland saw nothing in her that was broken.

"Good Lord, she's still looking!"

"Embarrassing, ain't it?" Suddenly the boy reached out
and messed up Leland's hairdo, a complicated arrangement that was parted on both sides. Each time he
moved—(this refers to Cecil)—the chains about his boots
gave off a chime. He had a package of cigarettes in the
pocket of his jacket and an identification bracelet that
weighed several pounds. His face was as disciplined and
unsmiling as a soldier's, but Lee could not very well see
the boy's expression when it was lost, as now, in morning
light.

There were other girls, other boys, too, all of them taking up their respective positions in his memory bank as he climbed the stairs. He stepped past Carl, the sole individual in the whole class who was smaller than himself. Lee liked him. Came next the boy called Smitty, and then a smattering of girls in shoes, socks, and pastel dresses cut in such a way as not absolutely to prevent a person from identifying that veinous little area behind each female knee. They were not thinking about him, certainly, these myriads of girls who preferred to be talking or smiling or, as the case may have been, pouting about something or another with their little faces. What he wanted really was to round up the mess of them and store them away in his pencil box.

They entered with solemnity and saluted the school's favorite teacher, an elderly person, mostly blind, easily confused by students exchanging names with each other or entering and leaving the room while walking backward. Lee particularly loved to see her take off her glasses and, bending near the script, squint at the list of names.

"James?"

Dorothy raised her hand. She was a brunette exhibit who weighed commensurately with her age and size. Her measurements were unimportant at that time, but fell within the range. Today her dress was violet and squeezed together at the waist—this done deliberately—with a sash of the same color. Of all the girls, Lee ranked her as perhaps the eighth or ninth prettiest, owing primarily to her hair, her calves, and her figure, thus far a potentiality only, but one in which he had great confidence.

She had also several pieces of kindred jewelry at chest, wrist, and her midnight hair.

"Will you read, please?" the teacher asked of her.

And did so, her voice spilling forward hastily over the words, which she treated as hindrances to be overcome.

He ranked her as possibly the third-most intelligent among the girls. Listening to her, he nearly fell off to sleep again—the previous night had been hard on him, and with but three hours of sleep to his credit, he was having trouble. Just then Preston handed a folded note to him and went through a series of facial expressions that mandated Lee to pass it along to the next person. It had come, that note, from the other side of the room, and was destined for a boy who sat near to the front. Lee watched as he unwrapped the message and then read it over with satisfaction. How, really, did it feel to receive a note like that from a girl like the one who had sent it?

Ten minutes went by. Across the way, Lee observed that Darlene had put her head down, and either had gone back to sleep again or else was trying to relieve the weight of her heavy black curls, now lying partly on and partly off the desk. The teacher meantime had left off speaking and was going slowly and confusedly through a pile of papers that she could not recall having ever seen before. The day had only just begun, and already Lee could feel the boredom moving up and down the room like a weather condition. Far away, a dog was yapping, while down in the street below a car was having trouble with its gears. Cecil, who sat just in front of Lee, alphabetically speaking, had arisen and, after striving in vain to get a view of the vehicle, began treading slowly backwards till he had vacated the room altogether.

It was the finest town in Alabama, and Leland could not be happier than if he had fallen to Earth in Montgomery or Birmingham, or places even more famous than those. He watched in admiration as Dwayne now also got slowly to his feet, stretched, and then headed off toward the boys' facility at the end of the hall. The class was getting smaller. Lifting her seventy-five-year-old head, the teacher looked out over the room, scanning, as it were, for lost scholars drifting out to sea.

The facility was crowded by the time Lee came to it, and he had no intention of trying to urinate within the hearing of Cecil and the others. And then, too, each cell already had a boy in it, each boy identifiable by his shoes or by the conversation they were carrying on with the poker players seated in the center of the room. Lee went at first to stand behind Cecil, but then changed his mind when he remembered that he was already too closely associated with that person in the public mind. Suddenly he jumped back, disconcerted to see some dozen or more dollar bills lying at hazard in the middle of the ring. School had been in session for but three weeks, and every day they were playing for larger and larger stakes. That was when Smitty glanced his way and studied him sadly for the space of several seconds.

"Lee?"

"Yes?"

"Want a coke?"

"Sure!"

"Okay, bring me one, too, okay?"

"Now?"

"Well, hell yeah, now! Tired of waiting."

Lee hopped to it. He had to thread his way between the poker players and then proceed down the row of framed dignitaries who lined both walls of the darkened hall. One would have thought the building vacant save for an opened room where an audience of girls sat staring up at the picture of a uterus etched on the blackboard in colored chalk. Here Lee stopped, turning his attention from the drawing to the girls. He could identify several persons in there, including a girl he had dated when he was nine. He nodded to her, and when that didn't produce anything, threw up his hand and waved. Which is to say until the teacher came and shut the door in his face.

Nothing surprised him anymore, neither girls nor teachers nor people willing to undervalue their own best memories. The day was not as new as just an hour ago, and the morning light now revealed just how many dust particles were adrift in the corridor—a very great many, indeed. In spite of the unimportance of such matters, this scene entered his memory where he foresaw that it would—but why?—forever remain.

He had to cross the street. The town, too, was empty, save for a few adults wandering purposelessly here and there—a woman with a child, a man, and others of that kind. Nor was the Teen Canteen (so-called) doing business at this hour. He entered nevertheless and, keeping his face to one side, addressed the rather hard-looking man who appeared to be looking back at him with the same kind of cynicism and disappointment that Lee was accustomed to seeing in Smitty and in the boy called sometimes "Lloyd" and sometimes Charlie T.

"May I have two Cokes?" he asked sweetly. He had the coins for it, but the man wasn't listening.

"Umm?"

"Two Cokes."

"Yeah, but you aren't even supposed to be here. Are you?"

"I'm going right back!"

"Does Mr. Morton know you're out here gallivanting around when you're supposed to be in class?"

"Not yet."

Lee watched as he gathered up two bottles and opened both of them with a device that was attached to the counter itself. Lee thanked him but had then to go back and hand over his quarter. Would he, or would he not, be given the change that was owing to him? At the back of the store a negro was delivering provisions of some sort, and meantime the jukebox was playing at high volume. Under circumstances such as these, it was altogether possible that Lee would get no change.

"Could I have my change, please?" he asked calmly.

A high school girl entered. Later on, looking back at her, he recalled her as a flaxen-headed creature, very cheerful (about five feet tall or more), and chewing gum. She was dressed in a light pink sweater and had a bracelet at her wrist and a brooch in her hair. Intimidated by the sight, Lee drew off into the shadows. She smoked cigarettes, this one, and had the sort of figure that was mostly lacking in girls of his personal acquaintance. Glad was he when finally, she abandoned the place.

"Could I have my change, please?"

"Umm?"

"Change."

The man produced it. "Don't want to see you in here again."

"No, sir."

The change was mostly in pennies, and although Lee had not far to go, yet it was difficult to travel with an opened bottle in each hand. Twenty yards into the trip, he actually dropped one of the containers (his own) and lost perhaps a fifth of the contents. Came then to him from various places the smell of honeysuckle, the sound of a train running through town, dogs barking, and several other measures of this particular moment in the history of civilization. But must he indeed go through life remembering *everything*? Suddenly he stopped and checked for his change, finding it intact.

He climbed the stairs. Bringing his unfortunate imagination into play, he had felt for the past fifteen or twenty seconds that he was perhaps the only person still left alive in all the world; instead, that moment, he perceived Lloyd loitering just next to the classroom where the mechanical drawing students used to meet. Lee sauntered over to him in the sort of lazy indifference that he had been practicing these last weeks.

"What, you in trouble again?"

"Yeah."

They shook. The boy's hand was larger than Lee's, of course, and had a quantity of chalk dust on it.

"How long do you have to stay out here?"

"I don't know. Don't care, neither. Shit, I just as soon be out here as . . . Hey, what you got there?"

"Coke."

"Okay, I'll have one of those."

Lee gave over one of the bottles, his own.

"Hey, this one ain't full!"

"Okay, I'll take it back then, if that's the way you feel," said Leland, his toughness showing.

"No, no, that's alright. What the hell."

They drank. Or rather it was Lloyd who did the drinking. Far away, down toward the end of the corridor, it appeared that one of the faculty might be watching. This person soon disappeared, however, into one of the rooms, and gave no further trouble. He needed no great length of time, Charlie, to finish off his Coke and give the bottle back to Lee.

"I got to get going now," Lee said, nodding toward the restroom where, as he believed, Smitty would be waiting with growing impatience.

"Pro-ceed, pro-ceed. Ain't nothing out here to do, that's for sure."

Lee thanked him and continued on. There was at this time a work of art on the restroom wall that portrayed a man and woman in sexual congress, an image so accurate (Lee assumed), so garish and well-drafted in three colors of chalk, that not even the janitor had had the heart to wash it off. Distracted by that, Lee did not at first fully appreciate that Smitty and the others had gone away. Dread came down on top of him. Someday, if not *this* day, he would be caught out in the open and given a beating for failing to deliver the promised Coke. On the other hand, the room was empty, and, if he were quick about it, he could urinate in peace. Thus Lee. He was standing in position, his eye on the art, his free hand clutching a bottle, and his mind beginning to fog over from last night's lack of sleep. That was when Carl entered and, finding Lee occupied, started to go back out again.

"It's okay," Lee reported. "I'm just about finished."

The boy returned. He was harmless and shy and, like most people, smaller and younger than those from the other side of town.

"What's going to happen to us, Lee?"

"I don't know. Just take it one day at a time, I guess."

The boy nodded and then went into one of the cells and locked the door, and soon after began to urinate in his own small and intermittent way. From outside they could hear the church bells suggesting it must be ten o'clock. Ten o'clock, and thus far no education had taken place in Alabama. From the window he watched as the bakery truck went past, an indication that the economy, at least, was continuing forward.

"Miss Beasley wants to know where you are. She knows you're not in class."

"So? Nothing surprises me anymore. Anyway, what do I care?"

"But she knows you aren't playing poker. I told her."

Lee thanked him. In any case, the class was almost finished, to judge by the hands of his Eisenhower watch. And then, too, his soft drink was getting warmer, all the more so as time went by.

"Want this Coke?"

The boy took it, sniffed it, and then very courteously set it on the window sill. He had rather to perish of thirst than contravene the rules.

They walked back together. He had expected (Lee) to be greeted by girls grinning appreciatively at his misconduct; instead, no one appeared to have noticed that he'd been gone. Meantime Cherise was standing and reading in her bright, clear, and rather theatrical voice that told a great deal about the sort of person she was. She was smart and tidy and well turned out, but Lee could see which of the girls had spiritual depth and which didn't. Truth was, he was in love with the brown-headed girl who sat behind Sonya Hunter. But by now it had come to that part of the day when the Sun reached the first three rows only, leaving the rest of the room in semi-darkness. Ensorcelled in the obscurity, Lee began to lapse into that mental state that came just about as close to actual sleep as could be managed under the circumstances. The teacher, too, was nodding off every once in a while, and then suddenly came awake again. No one wished to disrupt her. A note came by, this one addressed to Steven who, however, refused it. Such a strange silence now prevailed that Lee once again began to feel that he was dwelling in a ball of glass with many thick inches between himself and the world outside. He knew, of course, that something was wrong with him. These others, classmates of his, were normal people, but not so he who had to rehearse his gestures and facial expressions if he wished to have any sort of friendships and/or make a path through the world.

Noon did come, marked by the sound of bells, cars moving past, and dogs calling from the hills. According to regulation, he was to go downstairs and march direct to the cafeteria; instead, he fell in behind Cecil, where he could not be seen. In this position he found himself moving abreast with the boy called Travis, a large person with rotted teeth, said to be a Navy veteran. Lee put his age at about nineteen or more. They turned and looked at each other.

"Where're you headed?" the boy asked. "Over to the Canteen?"

"I'm going with Cecil."

"Well, where's he going?"

Lee shrugged recklessly. "I don't know. Canteen, I

guess."

But for Clarence, the yard itself was empty. That boy had been expelled the previous year, and now spent his time loitering about the building. Leland watched helplessly as the girls in their pastel dresses proceeded on toward the cafeteria where, had things been different, he might have joined them. It was a bright day, full of light and painted leaves and the scent of winter coming down from Tennessee. But must he also put this away in the storehouse of his all-too-cluttered mind?

Waiting until the last moment, they diverged, Cecil, Lee, and Travis from the line of march and dashed to the Canteen, already crowded with high school people. Music was playing, and he could see couples dancing in the back room. Suddenly he dug for his money, recollecting too late that he possessed just fifteen pennies. A tall girl was wearing lipstick and hose, her age about sixteen or more. By habit he then followed Cecil to the bar and waited as the boy ordered up a cheeseburger and Orange Drink. The food here was so far superior to that served anywhere else, he regretted sorely his lack of funds.

"What'cha having?" Cecil asked.

"Naw, I'm not hungry."

"Bullshit. What, you broke again? Give him a cheeseburger."

The man obeyed. (It was just two hours before that Leland had been commanded by this same individual never to reappear in this place.) And then, too, it was amazing to see the insides of Cecil's wallet, which had the paper bills in it that one might expect of an adult. The burger itself proved thick enough and had a wealth of fried onions on top.

"What d'you want to drink?"

"Well . . ."

"Give him an Orange Drink."

Lee accepted it, a frosty bottle that, placed on the floor,

would have come up to the level of his knee. The music had meantime changed over to Teresa Brewer, and the crowd had quieted somewhat to listen to it. He did not appreciate at that time, Lee did not, that it was 1950, and the town was going through a Golden Age of romance and music and life in a place where everyone knew each other.

He had hoped that they would *not* go into the back room, where it gave him a helpless feeling to see football players and boys with motorcycles dancing with girls in lipstick and hose.

"Let's go back here," Cecil instructed, making his way precisely into the back room. Lee shrugged. They were being followed by a Navy veteran of weak intelligence who also had invested in a cheeseburger and Orange Drink. It was dark in there, and he could see the faces of girls gleaming in the shadows. "I'm too young for this," said Lee to himself. "And yet, I feel pretty sure that Cecil won't let anything happen to me." Suddenly, just then, the music changed over to "Bonaparte's Retreat," an insidious piece that brought twenty couples out onto the floor. It would not have surprised him to see people kissing in the corners of the room, although nothing of that sort took place while he was actually watching.

"Look at that one," Travis said, pointing with his cheeseburger at a blasé-looking girl with a cigarette. "I wouldn't mind screwing that one."

Lee had expected it, language of that sort. He regretted that he had not gone on to the cafeteria.

"She's alright,"

"She's got a baby, is what they tell me."

Lee was appalled. He might be in the same school with her but was very far from wanting aught to do with babies at his age. He stretched and yawned, saying, "Well, maybe we better get on back."

"We just got here! What's the matter, Sloan?" asked Cecil, using his second-favorite appellation for the boy.

"You're not getting nervous on us again?"

"Not me."

"Hey, look at that one. Now that's a good-looking woman!"

She was, as said, exactly as Cecil described her. And then, too, she had a friendly way of dancing that resulted in her head resting against her boyfriend's chest. She was happy, perhaps sleepy as well, and was dressed in a red sweater that was as merry and vivid as the dimples that adorned her blameless face. Lee suffered. He had known this girl when she was a knock-kneed child of seven or eight. And if thus far the day had been a mediocre sort of thing, all that changed at once when she recognized him among the tables and smiled in his direction.

Lee put on a bored expression. He had been in this place a good five or six minutes, and although he was the smallest and youngest person there, no one so far had asked him to leave. Suddenly, that moment, the music changed over to the beautiful "Tennessee Waltz," Lee's favorite all-time piece. A thousand years might go by, and people would still be waltzing in Tennessee—such was his impression both then and thereafter as well. He watched as one of the high-school girls, his second-favorite, went out onto the floor and began to dance with Holly Parker, a high-quality basketball player and the best trumpet-player in town. Music filled the space, people were dancing and drinking drinks, and yet he had the certain feeling that in times to come no one would remember any of it save only he alone. He scarcely noticed when Travis gathered up his Orange Drink and decanted most of it into his own bottle. The veteran had a tattoo on his forearm showing an unclothed woman entwined in a python of some kind.

"You going to finish that cheeseburger?"

Lee gave it over to him. The music, to his grief, was coming down to an end, and with it some of the magic and luridness that invested the place. He realized then that Cecil was no longer with them and had in fact gone over to a group of girls where he could be seen chatting with them in his calm and pleasant style. He was as large as a man, almost, had money in his wallet and a pair of leather boots with chains on them. For one, brief moment, Lee actually thought of sauntering over to the same girls and loitering there alongside Cecil, which is to say until he came to himself and stayed where he was. It troubled him that Travis had taken out another cigarette and, after two or three efforts, had managed to ignite the match with his fingernail. Troubled him, too, that a policeman had come into the place and was scrutinizing the students one by one. Lee put on a cheerful and healthy expression. Having brought no books with him, he read his watch, saying, "Well, maybe we better get on back now."

"Watch this."

Lee watched, astounded to see the veteran bend forward and plant his glowing cigarette in the trouser cuff of one of the boys standing at the edge of the dance floor. He hoped to see the thing suffocate in there and cause no damage; instead a thin wraith of smoke immediately emerged and began to rise to waist-level where, however, it soon dissipated into the general red and purple murkiness of the place. The policeman had gone. Across the way, Cecil had picked up dancing with a girl whom Leland had not seen before, a milk-colored person in a virid-green sweater with bosoms in it. It was too much. He rose, stretched, and then made as if he were about to leave the place when, that moment, "Take Away the Breath of Flowers" came on, a new recording that he particularly liked and that seemed to represent this whole epoch in history and time. He didn't fully approve of these surroundings, and yet he knew that he was dangerously close to one of his "aesthetic experiences," as later he would call them, a mystical business that came to him from time to time when his system was overloaded with insights too hurriedly brought forth, as he later explained it, or too far prolonged as it were. If this were life and Leland could expect another seventy years of it . . . Well!

He waited for the moment to pass. There was such a wealth of girls in the place, all of them smiling and laughing, all of them tilting back and forth, eagerly pushed by natural law to fulfill their earthly missions. There had to be a reason for lipstick and eye shadow after all, for patent leather shoes and other methods of applying pressure on unsuspecting boys. Some, it is true, were to capitulate sooner than others. But what Lee could *not* understand, and never would, was how girls could operate that way in the first place. *They* were sweet and dimpled and fitted out in colored sweaters, whileas for the males, they were but box-shaped boys with noses and oversized feet. Thinking of it, he could feel himself losing some of his regard for the women and girls who sought male attention.

The larger part of that regard he still conserved, however. The girl called Barbara, for example, the leader of the majorettes—he regarded her so highly that he couldn't turn his gaze away. They lie, who say that girls weren't happy then; this one had been born for life and loved it to the hilt. It was while he was looking at her, lost in dreams, that suddenly a tall boy standing just next to the dance floor—it appeared that his pants cuff was on fire—began jumping up and down. He was torn, Lee, between laughing along with the crowd or keeping his eye on Barbara. Travis meantime had abandoned the café altogether while Cecil had disappeared into the "green room," so-called, a famous place where occasionally one could see silhouettes moving back and forth in candlelight.

He walked back in a state of excitement and despair. A thousand years might go by, but he'd still be just eleven years old. His wrists were so thin, and, truth was, he was intimidated, and not just by life but a great many other things as well. Nor could he talk to himself, not when he was approaching a building with faces in the windows. Instead he read his watch and, after putting on an annoyed expression, ran to catch up with Craig. Behind him, far away, a Hank Williams song could be heard coming faintly from somewhere.

"Hi," he said. "Cecil and I went to the Canteen."

"Figured you would."

"I had a cheeseburger myself. What did you have?"

"Anyway, you're not supposed to go over there."

"So what! So what if I'm not supposed to go?"

Craig didn't answer. His face was serious and full of concern. A thousand years might go by, and he'd never do anything.

"We were dancing, too."

The boy stopped. "Who with?"

Lee shrugged. They were coming close to the building, and there wasn't time for details. Three stories up, he saw Miss Beasley at her desk. Her lenses were thick and highly refractive and tended to conflict with windowpanes.

Lee reported to his locker and, after taking down his little clarinet, hurried off to the band room, where already Mr. Hudson was forcing the three flutists to go through certain measures that needed more work. It surprised Lee, it always did, to see that Cecil had somehow arrived there before him and was dithering with his trumpet, even going so far as to remove one of the valves and run his handkerchief through it. The seventh grade had six fine athletes, and all but one had chosen trumpets. Came then the half-dozen majorettes, pretty girls assigned to loiter in the back of the room in short pants. He nodded to Cherise, who nodded back. But with her it was simply a matter of common friendliness, whereas Lee could imagine the day when he might actually rise and go and talk with her, as when they had both been nine years old. Those days, lost in the confusions of time, would never come back again, as well he knew. The sixth athlete played drums.

He feared many things, Leland did, but mostly he feared the conductor, a vulpine man, intelligent to a fault, who had the authority to require people to stand and play their instruments in front of others. Lee, who would have preferred to take a beating from the Principal, tried to make himself as small as possible and just as invisible. It is true that he was surrounded by other clarinetists and oboe players, some of them with horns even squeakier than his own.

He was slow to assemble his instrument, a costly device comprising three segments of teak adorned with buttons and pads. Once fitted together, these elements formed a black cylinder of about two-thirds his own length. For three years and longer, he had been blowing into this thing, creating a nasal noise that expressed only too well his own social standing at that age. No one loved music more than he, and no one was as poor as he at producing any. Now, lifting the horn into position, it dismayed him to find that his reed had split down the middle and couldn't be used.

He had others, frail objects costing each thirty-five cents and more. Working with delicacy, he removed the ruined reed and slipped it into his breast pocket, where it would remain forgotten for the next year and three-quarters, till he found it by accident. All this was a tedious but necessary process, and by the time he had finished with it, the band was playing without him. Useless to try and catch up with them now.

The band had five trumpets in it, but he could always discern Cecil's from the others—a high screaming sound that seemed to come from a Roman army marching to the attack. Smitty's, on the other hand, was darker and deeper, heavier, more morose, elements of profundity in it, hopeless. Their music sorted well with the trombones, golden implements continually readjusting for size and pitch. These boys were larger than Lee and seemed to be in process of merging with their instruments, even sometimes becoming one person. Not so Carl, who was as much too small for his saxophone as Leland for his clarinet. And yet he was sometimes able, Lee, to give off a creamy sound that let him salvage his position in the band. Seen from a distance, he looked like a homunculus sucking on a pipe.

He could have mentioned the other players, too; instead, he lifted up his horn just in time to play the final measures. He didn't belong here, truly he didn't, he whose future, were he to have one, would pertain more to books than to music.

"Are you with us, Lee?" the conductor asked suddenly, turning his fierce gaze in Leland's direction.

"Yes, sir."

"Good, good. Got your little reed all nice and proper now?"

"Yes, sir. I think so."

"Excellent! I'm pleased." (The band members were grinning.) "And so does this mean that you want to continue to be a member of our little group, hm?"

"Yes, sir!"

"Or would you prefer Latin class? That's the choice, you understand."

"No, sir! Yes, sir, I want to stay here."

"Good! Good, good. That's real good Lee."

He was speaking to Lee but his attention and raven-like gaze had shifted over to Charlie T., who had set one of his cymbals off to one side and appeared to be picking at his nose. The majorettes meantime were lounging in the window where a person could esteem their suntanned legs. From somewhere came the sound of a truck laboring up a hill, and further, the noise of an airplane driving overhead. There on the floor, a splotch of sunlight was making its way ever so slowly toward two o'clock. Lee was not unacquainted with these moments, when the world is alert and sentient but time itself has stopped.

He returned to class to find that Cecil had arrived before him. This would have been the time for a nap, an interlude during which Lee could have refreshed himself with half an hour's worth of divine unconsciousness or one of his accustomed dreams. But no, the teacher, who appeared finally to have come awake herself, had gone to the front and was drawing problems in arithmetic on the board. He had seen this before, had Lee, having seen the precise same numbers in sixth grade. Must he indeed go through life allowing other people to catch up with what Craig and he and the others from his part of town had accomplished all those years ago?

He worked quickly through the list, copied it, and then passed the duplicate up to Cecil. In return, hidden as he was by the larger boy, Lee was almost never bothered by the teacher. His face, too, was generally innocent, whether he wanted it like that or not. He wore a long-sleeved shirt because his wrists were thin. He had fifteen cents in his pocket, a clarinet beneath his desk, and a cigar box with hardly anything in it. Such were his materials, apart from a fifty percent interest in a dog and the other usual things to be found in a person's home. Thinking of it, he managed to lapse off into a hypnogogic state in which he imagined he was actually sleeping in place. That was when a note came past, a voluminous message in Mattie's yellow ink. Meantime up front, Lois was suffering at the board with a piece of chalk in her hand. Her skirt was old and faded, her knees were stained with grass, and she was no better at maths than if she had been like Charlie T. Ended thus the hour and with it the eighteenth day of seventh grade as carried out in the Alabama of that day.

He walked home in the gathering gloom. Preston, dodging between the falling leaves, dashed past on his bicycle, followed by his wind-up dog. In the distance Lee discerned two girls, one in violet and the other red, both moving quickly homeward to turn in their reports. Their legs were thin but quick, and they were so obviously pleased to be out of school and in the September weather that Lee was tempted to race forward, scatter their books, and jump on top of them. It was to be the only time in his long life that he would happen to see the two of these in mid-gait at that particular location and time, and in fact he was at all times aware that everything he saw and did was to be done or seen but one time only, and then he'd be dead.

The gloom was not in the weather—it was only just past 3:30—but rather in the knowledge that he had only a specified time in front of him and then, as mentioned above, he'd be extinct or old or so corrupted by life that autumn days would mean nothing to him. He concentrated therefore on what was in front of him, striving to memorize it down to the least detail.

He had already memorized the houses along his way, as also the Roman wall that emerged up out of the ground for a few paces before disappearing underground again. He sighted Mrs. Ledbetter's home with the cat on the porch and the colored shutters, the movie theater and tobacco shop, and the Catholic Church with a sign out front showing a bleeding heart pierced by thorns. He passed slowly in front of Steven's house, formerly a friend of his. He had remembered the interior of that house and remained confident that he could still find his way through it in the dark. A mile to the east, he saw a crowd of birds circling by rote the town's faraway steeple.

He passed under Mr. Megan's pecan tree, conscious that all the nuts had long ago been harvested by others. (This same man had a plum tree out back, though none dared go there anymore.) Here, Lee halted, memorizing the roses before continuing on. History had been cumulating toward this moment, and he had but moments, parts of moments, before the world and everything would begin to spiral down into the mess to come. He was going to cross the street—he was sure of it—and sure, too, that he had no chance of reaching the other side. Gloom came down over him, and from a distance, he looked surprisingly like a little old man.

He entered the house at 3:58 and hurried to the parlor. The place was dark and ancient and had the most characteristic smell, somewhat like that of turpentine or camphor. He loved to get down on the rug and press his ear to the radio, a wooden appliance as big as the refrigerator almost. Entered then his mother, a good woman basically, who lately had taken on a physical appearance that looked like Lee's. She brought wafers and milk and then left him to deal with the radio on his own. A thousand years might go by and never once did Lee question these privileges of his. As to the adventures of *Jack Armstrong, the All-American Boy*, he recognized in them a foretelling of his own future career in the world. The broadcast, coming from New York, was perfectly audible, and made it possible for him to memorize whole paragraphs of the spoken script. But for certain particulars, they might almost have been talking about him.

It was the best part of the day. Lying on his back in the darkened room, he waited for *Sky King*, the on-going story of an aviator and a girl called Penny whose voice and general personality were very like those of some of the girls of Leland's acquaintance. Outside, the Sun was streaming, breeze blowing, dogs barking, and children calling up and down the street. They were good, programs like these, and he was at all times conscious of the top-most position of his own state when compared alphabetically with the rest. Thinking of it, he began to exult in his unseemly manner.

It had required a thousand years to arrive at this, and while he was grateful to the people of the past, some of them, yet was he also perhaps a little bit arrogant for having chosen *this* time and place instead of *theirs*.

He was deep into the program called *Inter Sanctum* when, suddenly, the afternoon began to lapse into twilight, a transformation so subtle that only those watching very keenly could have noticed. He saw the first firefly working its way bravely through the colloids, a tentative insect indeed, its lantern brief and dim. Using his Will, Lee tried to bolster him somewhat while at the same time giving heed to the radio and a woman trapped in an empty house.

They feasted that night on spare ribs and sauerkraut, Lee, the woman, his father, and tiny brother. As to the man (called "Young Albert" among the family), he was tired and had been at work all day. Lee waited until his father had served himself, had cut a portion, and had begun to chew upon it with approval. The room itself was dim—they preferred it that way—and no noises could be heard apart from the serious and static-filled sound of news from the radio. The political situation was bad, as Lee divined from the way his father went on listening to it with deepening concern. Someone meantime was trudging down the alley that ran behind the house, whereupon Leland's father rose suddenly and snapped the curtains shut. The milk was good and plenty of it; no one in *this* house would starve tonight.

He loved these moments. The curtains were tied, and in case the telephone sounded, it was to be ignored. His mind, Lee's, attached itself to his father's revolver, a blued article that lay half-buried among the pajamas and nightgowns that filled the top drawer. And was there anything in that house that he could not have located to within an inch of its position? No. No, he knew about the business papers, the box in the attic, his mother's necklace, and a

great many other things as well. They had books, they had
guns, they had canned fruits and vegetables, and six hundred dollars in the bank.

All this was owing to the adults, which tended to un-
derwrite his general obedience to them. Both these people
were a little bit faded at this hour, and he fully expected
his father to repair very soon to the parlor where he would
smoke two, sometimes three cigarettes while listening to
the radio. Lee made haste to assist with the dishes, which
is to say until he saw that it was something his mother
could deal with individually.

The parlor: The news was finished and a crime show
had come on. Unwilling to stretch out on the floor in his
father's presence, Lee, wearing an expression as serious as
Young Albert's, sat upright in the upholstered chair. His
brother had long ago disappeared from the kitchen—
where did he go during these intervals?—but now was
back for a second bowl of ice cream. Suddenly shots rang
out over the radio, and Lee could clearly hear the sound of
someone running down a corridor. His father, too—he
had put down his newspaper and was harkening to the
program. No one hated crime more than he, and no one
yearned more for information leading to the capture and
conviction on a regular schedule of bad people. The
smoke from his cigarette lifted ever so slowly and filled
the lampshade that held it there. He was a melancholy
man, and his memory was as deep and as full as Lee's, if
not more so indeed. That was when Leland's pale brother
emerged from the kitchen and, after shaking hands with
the old man, ran off to bed.

It was a privilege, staying awake till nine at night, and
one that Lee exploited to the lees. He had done his
homework five hours ago, having done it in his head while
trekking home from school. The world was disturbed with
issues and struggles of all kind, but for him the main thing
was to stay for the next program, a dark business having

to do with a rocket trip to the Moon.

He slept that night between fresh sheets. Or *tried* to sleep, rather, and even at one moment came so close to it that he was momentarily persuaded that he was actually dreaming. His stratagem was to insert himself by imagination into one of those cliff-side apartments used by the Pueblo Indians, complex structures in which a person could move from room to room, sometimes sleeping and sometimes visiting other people; instead, he found himself staring at somersaulting shadows cast on the wall by passing cars. He tried then to imagine himself on board a submarine parked at the bottom of the sea. Or, that he was dwelling with his wife in a stockade in French Canada with snow on the ground and wild Indians all about. Or, that his body parts had been disassembled and put away in a carton, like pencils in a box. Instead, his mind, which had a life of its own, went on running forward, jumping over creeks and other obstacles and pausing only for girls and mathematical problems and tattered hearts embedded in barbed wire.

At 11:30 he arose, gathered his flashlight and stamp album, and tiptoed over to the roll-top desk, an inheritance from his grandfather that took up a large percentage of the room. That desk had six drawers in it, each filled with objects and other things organized by Lee in his fastidious manner. So persnickety was he indeed that instead of fingers, he was wont to use a sharpened pencil, and sometimes even a set of tweezers to coax things into proper place. He admired straight lines and ninety-degree angles and couldn't bear to see things out of skew.

His album was blue, had a coat-of-arms on the cover, and contained 2,437 non-duplicated stamps, approximately speaking. It is true that the world's nations were by no means equally represented in his collection, not as long as he gave preference to places that were strange and far away and inscribed in some of the odd-looking scripts

found in Asia and elsewhere. Chinese! in which every single letter looked like an obscenity, or like an infant's version of an authentic word. The men, on the other hand
(the men on the stamps), looked to be in deadly earnest.
He didn't understand them, Lee didn't. What did they
want? And what was that building in the background, the
one with the spires? And that landscape of hills and
mountains that, apparently, was designed to appeal to the
sort of Chinese people who stood in need of stamps?

Running forward to the middle of the album, he
trained his flashlight on Persia, the most peculiar by far of
all the world's countries. These people had originated the
practice of embossing their stamps in silver and gold, an
expensive indulgence that, insofar as he knew, had been
followed by no other country. But mostly it were the kings
that fascinated Lee, generation after generation of some of
the most corrupt-looking beings ever seen. And then his
favorite stamp of all, a pale-yellow affair showing a sleepy-
looking Shah dressed in a preposterous hat. Next to this,
his collection of French colonies was of but secondary interest.

It did calm him, he admitted it, the postage of Mauri-
tania showing a native oarsman pushing upriver in the
ink-black night. One could imagine the mosquitoes in an
environment like that, the crickets, and the monkeys yell-
ing from tree to tree. Coming closer, he believed that he
could discern a crocodile lurking at the river bank. Suddenly he stopped, alerted by the sound of his father mill-
ing about in the further rooms.

He had enjoyed thirty minutes of pretty good sleep,
followed by ten or fifteen more of somewhat lower quality
when, that moment, Chichi Roberts, a neighboring boy
who lived on the corner, burst into his room and began
shaking him violently.

"Lee! Lee!"

Lee looked at him and then, slowly, got into a sitting

position. Once more he was reminded of how strange it was that while his father always kept the curtains closed, yet he never locked the door.

"Lee!"

"What!"

"You got any graph paper?"

The dog also had come awake.

"Yeah. A little bit."

"Can I borrow one?"

"Gollee, you *still* haven't done your homework?"

"Forgot."

"Aw, good Lord. I did mine a *long* time ago."

"And what are all those stamps over there?"

Lee hurried over and closed the album. He had five sheets of graph paper and wasn't opposed to sharing one of them.

"I'll pay you back," Roberts claimed.

"Doubt it."

"Hey!"

"Naw, it's just my brother. He always sleeps like that."

"Well. See you tomorrow, I reckon."

Lee nodded and then went to the window and opened it enough to let the boy escape. Ended thus the twenty-third of September, even less education having taken place in Alabama on that day than all the days before.

Three

He woke at four o'clock, got into his shoes, and then, seeing what time it was, got back into bed. He believed that he might actually be able to go to sleep again, provided he were able to place himself mentally in the right circumstances—on board a submarine, for example, or a well-built cabin in the French-Canadian wilderness with danger all about. This succeeded at last, and after finishing with Canada, he envisioned himself in the Captain's quarters of a seventeenth-century sailing vessel standing off the coast of Siam. He knew that he was dreaming, of course. Even so, smacking his lips over it, he retreated under the covers and permitted this and other dreams to carry him through till seven o'clock.

Coming from separate rooms, they gathered at the table and waited for the woman to seat herself. Lee couldn't fail to see that his father had a daub of shaving cream beneath his chin; however, it wasn't the time to remind him of it. The man hadn't had his coffee yet, and meantime the radio was sputtering badly. Moreover, the little bit of news that came to them was about the Soviet Union. Lee reached for the toast and jelly and, putting on a concerned face, ate a good part of it before his mother pointed him back to the oatmeal. Very soon now, his brother would be spilling orange juice down his bib and, often as not, into his lap as well, a tradition the family was too courteous to mention.

He loved these smells, Lee, of coffee, grits, and eggs. They mixed with the other indefinable scents that invested the house and seemed to be implicit with it. A thousand years might go by, it would still smell the same. With the curtains shut, the four people now bent over their meal with renewed seriousness, aware at all times that in other parts of the world there was no food at all. A plane flew over, fouling the radio waves. Far away, a dog was grieving in the hills, while from town itself there came the sound of bells warning of the dangers of a brand-new day.

He went a quarter of a mile without treading upon a single crack and then halted and began rummaging through Mrs. Person's persimmon tree, finding not a single fruit. Preston dashed past on his bicycle, chased by a small, square dog on inch-long legs. He saw men in automobiles, all of them heading off to places where they must spend the next eight hours in the sort of useless confinement that had put Lee in fear of growing up. It was bad enough, life, without having to work for it. If he were lucky, he might run down Sonya Hunter on her way to school, and if not lucky, might run into a spate of eighth-grade boys who would want to rob him of his lunch. He stopped to check his wallet, his homework, and pencil box, finding everything intact.

Today it was Sonya Hunter. He hurried and managed to catch up with her at the intersection,

"Hi," he said in his indifferent way.

"Hi." She was a well-presented individual of Lee's favorite size and type. In her case, however, she wore a blue dress with a velvet collar of some kind and a belt with a silver buckle. He understood perfectly why girls were as insane about clothes as they were, owing to the effect.

"Get your homework done?"

"Most of it."

"Most of it? Shoot, I did mine in five minutes!"

The girl said nothing. He thought he saw a trace of annoyance cross her heart-shaped face and decided to pursue it.

"I don't know why you people have so much trouble with your homework. It's easy!"

"Well, what about you! Maybe that's why nobody likes you, did you ever think about that?"

"Cecil likes me."

"Oh, Cecil. Nobody else."

"Smitty likes me."

"Well, sure, *he* likes you! He'd like anybody."

"No, actually, he hates most people."

"Well, no wonder."

Lee laughed, or tried to. He could hardly believe that at one time, before he'd gone bad, this girl had been an exceptionally good friend of his. Thinking of it, he fell into the moroseness that was nearly always the aftermath of his affiliations with girls.

"Remember that old crate that was in your back yard?

We used to play in there sometimes."

The girl said nothing.

"We were in the third grade at that particular time."

He saw a second look of annoyance that was very like the first.

"We weren't going steady, or anything like that."

"No."

"We could have been, but we weren't." And then: "Marlene is going with Steve right now."

"I know."

Preston, hoping to usher his dog back home again and still arrive at school on time, hurried past on his bicycle. Lee waved to him and then turned to the girl in his insouciant way.

"You're not going with anybody at this particular time, are you?"

She agreed that she was not. They were moving past a landscape of deep lawns and expensive homes that seemed to be looking down their noses at them. Certainly, the economy was good in these areas, better even than it ought to be, according to his preternatural instinct in these matters. The girl, too, came from a good economy, whileas for the people in passing cars it must have seemed that she had become "his girl" once again. He knew better than to ask to carry her books, however.

"We have a horse," Lee said suddenly. "Actually, it's my horse, but we keep him on a farm. Want to go riding someday?"

Her eyes brightened.

"And then we could start going together again. If that's what you want."

Her eyes dimmed. They were moving through the poor section, Lee at all times appalled by the possessions (a ruined sofa, an upside-down washing machine) that sat at random in the yards. People were stagnating on their porches, and through the open doors one could see into the hallways and out into the open field that bordered the town on that side. Money was scarce, for those as didn't have some already. And how about this, that the less one needed it, the easier it was to get. They passed a garbage can lying on its side—no one cared—a battered item disgorging coffee grinds and other sorts of filth out into the road. Neither Sonya nor Lee had anything to say about this, understanding, as they did, that it wasn't polite to talk about people.

"There's going to be a *dance* on Thanksgiving," Lee said suddenly. "That's what they claim, anyway."

The girl didn't speak.

"You going?"

"I haven't decided."

"Me neither, I haven't decided neither. I might."

Far away they heard the 7:45 bell, a portentous noise that came from the Episcopal building down on Ninth Street. Lee turned and checked on his brother, following palely at a remove of about two hundred yards. Otherwise, it promised to be a pretty good day. The Sun was large and spotless, and Lee had accrued a good five, possibly six hours of medium-grade sleep.

"Well if you don't go to the dance, what *are* you going to do?"

"Oh, I'm sure I can find a way to pass the time."

"Yeah, but . . ."

"We might go to Florida."

He could feel his gorge rising. Every time he saw her, she seemed to have become prissier.

They came to school in time to loiter about for a few minutes before the klaxon summoned them inside. Lee looked for Cecil and, failing to find him, went and stood next to Craig, a part-time friend of his whose father was employed in the same occupation as Lee's. Suddenly he realized, Lee, that Cecil was standing off to one side with Gwendolyn, who was much more beautiful at that time than fated to become later on. "Good Lord!" he said, moving a step or two in their direction. They were so near, their twenty toes were almost touching one another. Lee worked his way around to the other side, where his view was clearer and had fewer people in the way. Dressed as she was in a grey skirt and a scarf that had been chosen deliberately, she comprised the perfect match for Cecil, who had just the height for her. And then, too, he had an identification bracelet made of massy links that weighed a great deal. Came then to mind a famous saying that Lee had heard, namely that "the greater the distinction between boys and girls, the happier girls and boys will be." That was when the klaxon sounded.

But time was passing, and he had less than one hundred fifty seconds before he'd have to climb the stairs and sit in place for the next several hours. Accordingly, he ran to the boys' room and had managed to urinate almost to completion before one of the ninth graders came in.

"Hi!" Lee said, getting no reply from the boy, a red-headed individual of about twice Lee's size. It intimidated him, the way these people could pee in plain open view without the least nervousness. That was when Smitty came in and, taking up the adjoining position, began also to urinate while standing shoulder to shoulder with the red-headed boy, his own worst enemy.

"Hi!" Lee reiterated, waiting to see if these two would begin smiting each other with their free hands. No, they finished up quickly and went their ways, all except Smitty, who stayed behind with Lee.

"You been helping Cecil, hadn't you?"

"Little bit."

"Math, stuff like that."

"Yeah."

"Well, shit, how come you ain't helping *me*?"

"I figured Craig was helping you."

"Craig, shit, he's even stupider than me!"

"Naw, he's not anywhere *near* as . . ." He stopped.

"Besides, I ain't got time for all this shit."

"Me, neither! Shoot, I have to practice, I have to mow the lawn, I have to . . ."

"Practice what?"

"Clarinet."

"That's not what I hear. You hadn't practiced in *years*, is what I hear."

That was true.

"And besides, I have to go to ballroom lessons on Saturdays."

"Go what?"

"Ballroom."

"Great God A'mighty. I never know what you're going to say next!"

"Hey, we got to hurry or we're going to be late."

"I'd like to go to one of these ballrooms someday," he said in dreamy fashion. "See what y'all do in there all the time."

He had taken out a cigarette, but then had put it back when he remembered the time. Lee had expected and had hoped that the bell would already have rung by now. He waited briefly as Smitty again took out a partial cigarette and began making preparations to urinate for a second time within the past two minutes and a half.

Truth was, he preferred, Lee, the more civilized ambiance of a room with girls in it. His teacher had bad eyes, but Lee even so felt pretty sure that no one would attack him or take his books as long as she still held any sort of sway over the place. Moving slowly (he was late), he broached up to his desk and slipped in behind Cecil, who appeared still to be in a "Gwendolyn" mood, as it were. Lee bent forward and whispered at him.

"I saw what you were doing with Gwendolyn."

The boy reddened, but declined to turn around.

"I thought you were going with Beth! You said you

were."

From outside came the sound of several things, including especially that of a plump brown bird who had taken up a stance on the windowsill and was reproving, as it almost seemed, the twenty-six students. Shielding his mouth, Cecil hissed back at Lee without turning around.

"I'm going with Gwen now."

"Yeah, but . . . !"

"Besides, it hadn't got anything to do with you, anyhow."

That was it. Henceforward, the boy could do his own mathematics, and Lee, who would never have a chance with Gwen, was free to look upon Beth in a new light entirely. That was when a message came by, a two-page affair in yellow ink. Lee passed it on and then, seeing that the teacher was looking in his direction, put on an expression of maturity and concern. It distracted her from Smitty, who moved slowly from his desk to the door and then from door to hall. The bird had gone. Lee observed then how the Sun was running through Ramona's fine brown hair that scintillated every few seconds in sparks of gold. It distressed him that she was again wearing what looked like a set of her father's cast-off shoes, and that her ankles were as thin and muddy as they were. Except for those, he had warm feelings for her. Thinking of that, he felt as if he might be able to hunker down in Cecil's shade and recoup a few moments of sleep.

This day, he hoped to cross to the cafeteria along with the others; instead, that moment, Cecil came up behind and began steering him to the Teen Canteen.

"Where you think you going, Sloan?"

"We're going to get in trouble."

"Then I guess you might just as well go on back home and climb into bed. Is that what you want?" And then: "You get that math done?"

He had done the math and the civics, too, and today

the Canteen was running over with laughter and music. Putting on his expression, Lee now pushed his way inside and began to work his way between the high school girls in their perfume and sweaters and, in some cases, their cigarettes. He was under the influence of these people, already he was, and the corruption was beginning to show in his face. And as if that weren't already too much, the jukebox now once again was playing "Bonaparte's Retreat," a popular song of the times that should never have been allowed into public circulation. A fat man in an apron was cooking hamburgers on the grill, and by the time Lee came to the head of the line, the fellow was at the end of his patience.

"Yeah?"

"Nothing," Lee said, remembering at the last moment that he had brought no money. "Never mind."

"You people, you come in here. Say, how old are you, by the way, hm?"

He could feel himself, Lee, getting confused. Where was Cecil? Meantime the music had come down to the lewdest part of the whole piece while Lee, his eye continually adjusting to the dark, had begun to make out the silhouettes of people dancing in the adjoining room. Suddenly he plunged for his money, coming out with but a single dime and two pennies, one of them lead. He could leave this place and not come back, a thought that came to him in an inspiration of delight. And that, of course, was when Cecil came up behind, took him by the collar, and whispered seriously into his right-hand ear.

"I got to watch you every minute of the day—is that what it is? Here, take it, take it, take it."

Lee took it, an American silver quarter that appeared to be almost new. Never would he understand it, how these boys from the other side of Noble Street disposed of so much money. On this occasion, Lee ordered a cheeseburger and Orange Drink and, after waiting with an ex-

pression of final impatience for the man to pry off the cap,
went to the same table as yesterday. From this vantage
one could see what was happening, both on the floor and
in the "Green Room," so-called, where the sixteen- and
seventeen-year-old junior and senior girls were largely to
be found. The music had meantime switched over to a
Teresa Brewer song—even given the chance, he wouldn't
want to leave the place while this one was singing—Teresa
Brewer. He saw two football players wearing jerseys with
numbers on them, and then the boy called Clarence who
had been expelled last year and now spent his days washing dishes in the Canteen or loitering about the grounds.
Where was Cecil?

Suddenly, he perceived two high school girls at the
next table who seemed to be smiling at him in a maternal
sort of way, whereupon Lee went quickly over into a fresh
expression that made him look even younger and smaller
than he was. That was when a policeman entered, a large
man with a baton and a hat with a glossy bill. Lee, who
had never wanted to be present during any of the knife
fights that sometimes went on here, was pleased to see
him. Pleased, too, when the very beautiful "Tennessee
Waltz" came on. It had an effect upon the girls, that music, making them *prettier* as it were, and more prone to
dancing he would have said, and more vivid withal. From
out of his future readings this thought came down to him:
that girls do have a mission in life and are impatient, most
of them, to make a start on it. It was that moment there
came to him the following voice: "Hi, cutie pie."

Lee froze. Where was Cecil? He hadn't forgot there
were two high school girls at the next table, nor forgot
that they had been smiling at him. *This*, however, he had
never expected.

"Cutie pie. I'm talking to you."

He declined to look at them. Instead, taking up his Orange Drink, he drank deeply, his face exposing a bored

expression. He was only eleven years old, and these twelfth graders, as he reckoned them to be, would quickly tire of him, he supposed.

"Okay, cutie pie, I already told you once to come on over here. I'm not going to tell you again."

His hand and knees began to tremble. And where was Cecil when he most was needed? Even now he could have leapt up and run outdoors, and would have done so except for the Orange Drink. At last, he turned and looked the girl full in the face, the first time he had done so. She had long hair and lipstick—his vision clouded over—and was beautiful in every way.

"Are you coming?" she asked. "Or not?"

"No," Lee said quickly, looking off into another direction. "Don't have time."

"Don't?"

"No, ma'am."

He heard laughter. There were now three or four tables paying attention to him, all of them grinning in his direction. He drank hurriedly, hoping to finish the stuff before it was too late. Outside, he saw a group of boys of his own size and type moving past happily, all of them free of the sort of pressures that hung over him. The girl now stood— she was as tall as a woman—and began moving toward him. Lee hummed. Sometimes he could make himself think of other subjects, of books he had read, or stamps and films.

But of all those things, the very last he had expected was for the girl to take up a handful of his hair and pull him into the standing position. Lee stood, looking off into the same direction in which he had looked before. Something was about to happen. It surprised him even more when the girl then forced his head back in such a way that he was actually looking up at the ceiling. Her face was near and beautiful and her perfume so sweet that he didn't know what to do. He observed the face grow nearer still, and then testified that she was kissing him full on the lips. No sleep tonight! He could hear laughter coming from several places. A little more of this and his neck began to tire, such was the angle. It came then to him that he might actually suffocate. "I've never done anything like this before," he said. "But now I have." Opening his eyes, he discovered Cecil standing off at a distance, his face full of surprise.

"Good God A'mighty," the boy said. "I can't leave you alone for five minutes!"

The girl meantime had drawn back and was asking, "Did you like that, cutie pie? Just a little bit?"

"No!"

Laughter. He was being examined by forty eyes.

"You'll like it plenty," one of the boys said, "when you're a little bit older."

"He likes it now. Look at him."

"Hell, I been trying for *years* to get her to do that to me."

He had been the center of attention for perhaps two minutes and already they were beginning to turn away, a pattern that would follow him to the end. Someone had taken his drink.

The balance of that day passed in a haze of conceitedness and shame. His standing with Cecil had improved markedly, but when he tried to describe things to Craig and the others, no one believed him. "You aren't supposed to talk about stuff like that," Cecil explained. "It's private."

"Yeah, well, what about you! And what about Gwen!"

"That's private, too."

"Yeah, but . . ."

"So don't talk about it. They don't like that, girls don't."

"Oh."

He was learning a great deal, he thought, about kisses and girls.

He slept that night between ironed sheets and then emerged at just after ten to check on his stamps. His collection needed a lot of work, but after twelve minutes during which he found himself thinking about other things, he got into his shoes and trousers and exited by way of the window. The Moon was large and white and had a circumference that was particularly well-defined on this occasion. It also served to reveal Mr. Jenson, a garrulous man, sitting on his front porch. He must be careful here, Leland, lest that person discern him in the dark and telephone his parents. Thus Lee, who could not fully relax until he had moved around the corner and had disappeared.

God, he did so love the night. It was as if everyone had died, and history was over, and he alone was left to try out different homes and go into department stores. Moving on tiptoes, he descried a weak lamp glowing greenly in the woods, whereupon he had an aesthetic experience on the spot. From someone's radio, he heard a familiar voice reporting the last news of the day, a hasty summary that would have to suffice until tomorrow. He saw then that the light in Mildred Weston's bedroom had not yet been extinguished, a sign that that most studious of all girls was still bending over her homework at 10:45 in late September.

He cheered for her, for all girls everywhere in 1950. Suddenly, just then, he saw that an automobile had turned into the street and was trundling slowly in his direction. Posting himself behind a shrub, he waited till the vehicle was even with him and then began running alongside the driver, a stunt that seemed to horrify the person and almost sent the car off into Mr. Lauren's yard. He told himself that he needed to remember to tell Cecil about it later on.

His heart was more powerful and his head so much more functional at night that he couldn't understand why civilization had chosen to operate in consonance with the

Sun instead of the other way around—a mistake. And then, too, nighttime was so good at covering up the little flaws and bare spots that afflicted even the best of times in even the best of cities. That said, and feeling as he did that he had pretty well finished up with this evening's exercises, he began cautiously to reflect back upon the dying day, a lengthy project culminating in a kiss.

Four

Came Saturday, he had an engagement with a friend whose dog had just turned two years old. Getting slowly into his white suit, his cologne, and a bowtie with the picture of a trout on it, he left home at just after lunch and walked the four blocks to where Preston dwelt amid a cluster of two- and three-story homes with double-glazed windows, where the economy was unusually strong at this time. He carried, Lee, a gift wrapped in blue paper and, in his pocket, a folding knife with a handle made of bone.

He had not gone half the distance before he began "woolgathering," his mother called it. These houses, this neighborhood, they were exactly like the place where he himself had dwelled some thousand years ago or more, in that "other domain" that seemed to be pressing on him more and more as he grew older. But mostly it was the strangeness of things, and the certain feeling that he could have poked holes in the encompassing panorama and peeped out into the void. Or rather, that life was a drama being staged for his benefit alone, an act of generosity on the part of those who wanted to support his illusions for as long as they could. Indeed, he could imagine stagehands and set designers running back and forth to organize the scene.

Today, the world comprised a tidy and well-built neighborhood with two- and three-story homes full of girls and servants and high-grade furniture. He stepped past the sculpture of a negro picking cotton and then turned and bowed sweepingly to an actual negress house-cleaner in a bandana, watching between the curtains.

He climbed the steps and rang the bell. He waited for Preston's mother, and when she had opened for him, put on an innocent and wholesome expression as he handed over his gift.

"Yes, ma'am," he said, "we thought it would be real nice of us to get something for Ringo."

She laughed. She was a tall woman with a necklace and a hairdo, both of them appropriate enough, perhaps, for the forty- or maybe the fifty-year-old she actually represented. He had no quarrel with these people, however, or anyway not while she was smiling at him in that motherly way that made him wish he had brought a gift for her as well.

"And who is that?" she asked, referencing a small person lagging some hundred yards behind.

"Aw, that's just my brother. He's not invited."

He knew the general layout of this building, and although he was far from having seen *all* the rooms, he could quickly trace to its source the sound of laughter and squealing. It was irrational of him, of course, to think that a certain high school girl might also have come. Instead, he entered with an expression of mild annoyance and strode direct to the dog who had been dressed in a paper hat held on with a string. So far, Lee had not bothered to determine which humans might or might not be present.

"Lee!" someone called. But even then he did not turn around. The dog was excited and seemed to understand this was his special day. Had the dog been Leland's instead of Preston's, he would have been a German Shepherd or something of that sort.

"Lee!"

"What!"

"Brenda is here."

It was true; already he had caught view of her sitting in
the corner with two other girls who were much less well-
known to Lee than she. "I see," said Lee to himself. "They
think we're still going together, Brenda and me." Speaking
out loud, he said, "What y'all doing?"

"Playing cards. You want to play, too?"

"Depends." After his experiences, it seemed almost too
genteel to him, cards. Even so, he came reluctantly, and
after studying the routine, decided to join them. That was
when it occurred to him to take out some money and set
it in the "pot."

"Hey! We aren't playing for money!"

The game had five people in it, most of them girls. He
glanced at the one in the aquamarine dress, not certain
whether she disliked him or whether that was admiration
in her face. Bored already, Lee drew back his money and
put it away.

"We *always* play for money," he said. "Cecil and me."

"Oh, Cecil!"

Long ago and far away, his mind began to drift. It was
then that Preston's mother came and took up a position
on the divan, as they called it, pretending she were interested in what they were doing. She wore a large smile to
prove what a good time they were having.

"And how are your parents, Lee? I haven't seen them in
so long."

"Good."

"And your father. I don't know anyone who grows prettier roses than your father."

"Yes, ma'am. He won a prize." (He could see halfway
up her dress, such was the position she had assumed.)

"No! You must be so proud."

Lee thought about it. Now that she mentioned it, he
did begin to feel somewhat proud. "Yes, ma'am. And he
caught two catfish, too."

She wasn't listening. Her chief concern was for the cake

and ice cream, and whether these had been properly arranged on the table along with the doilies and noise makers and wooden spoons.

"And how about you Lee? We so wanted Linda to be here, too." (She smiled knowingly.)

"Yes, ma'am. Actually, we aren't going together at this particular time."

"Oh?"

She wasn't listening. The maid had fetched her a telephone with a very long cord, giving her the chance to speak to someone her own age. Lee waited as the conversation went on, not certain whether his interview was over already. Across the room, Reese and George had gotten into a struggle which they were trying to conduct in silence. He had no chance, George, but Lee couldn't fail to be impressed by the effort. He glanced in Brenda's direction, coming away with the distinct feeling that she had been staring at him. And yet he had no great wish to restore relations with her, not after the rather gloomy business of last year. Instead, he glanced to Preston's mother. She was wearing hose of some sort, and where she was sitting, a person could see the upper reaches where the nylon turned from sheer to brown.

They were having lots of fun—such was the consensus, anyway. Feeling that he might be in danger of becoming bored, Lee turned to Bethany, a golden-headed girl good at cards.

"Cecil is going with Gwen now," Lee said, watching her closely.

"Good."

"Good? He used to be going with *you*!"

She put down her cards. "I don't care *who* he's going with. And besides . . ."

Lee waited for the remainder of the statement which, however, never came.

"I guess she's just about the prettiest girl in school," Lee went on, rolling his eyes in dreamy fashion. "Whew!"

That was when Preston came in, entering the conversation from twenty feet away: "She's okay. But Barbara's even prettier, if you want my opinion."

"Aw, good Lord!" Lee could feel his gorge rising. "Just because she's got those dimples? So what! And besides, Cecil used to go with her, too!"

"Sure. Until she broke up with him."

"She did *not* break up with him. He broke up with her."

"No, *she* did. Her mother made her."

That was possible. Lee sat again, admittedly relieved not to have to get into a fight with the host of the party who, in any case, had more allies in the immediate vicinity. Meantime he had lost three consecutive hands and was becoming bored with the game. His face reflected that. And this: would there, or would there not, come a time for cake and ice cream and for dancing in the dark?

He stood and, while standing, finished off his goblet of sherbet. The room was paneled in dark wood and contained a series of Civil War etchings in the same corner as the pool table. Lee sauntered in that direction and then sidled up to Michael, who had been studying the drawings very seriously over the past few minutes.

"What is that, Bald Ewell?"

"Yeah."

"What, they getting ready for ———?"

"Naw, you're thinking about Longstreet. Ewell was just a Brigadier then."

"Wait a minute—that looks like Cleburne!"

"Yeah. He got killed."

"Killed at Franklin."

"Right. We would of won if he hadn't got killed."

"We would of won if Jackson hadn't got killed, too."

"I know it."

They came nearer. These people had a tragic look to them, as if they had always foreseen that no army could stand up to odds of thirty-to-one.

"We killed a lot more of them than they killed of us."

"Yeah. But they had a lot more soldiers than we did."

"Sure, but what *kind* of soldiers? That's what matters."

Reese came up. A minute ago he had pinned George to the floor, but even so had come away with a couple of scuff marks on him. He checked the etching and then took off his glasses and bent nearer to it.

"Kill 'em all!" he said. "We should of killed every last one of 'em when we had the chance."

"We will. Next time."

"Burn 'em out!"

"Yeah." Lee could see the coals gleaming in Reese's eyes. Was it feasible? To go back from 1950 and do it over again? Lee looked for but was unable to find anyone there who wasn't willing to try.

He had been wrong about the ice cream—they were given as many helpings as they wanted, at the end of which time the music came on and the lights went down. He was grateful to the boy's mother for that, who seemed to believe they were too naïve to fully appreciate what it (dancing in the dark) truly was. And then, on top of that, and as if the day had not already been well above average, the first tune they played was "My Foolish Heart," his favorite in the world. It was too much, the dread combination of darkness and that song. He ran to Darlene, getting there before anyone.

"Want to dance?" he asked, taking her arm just above the elbow and guiding her onto the floor. This was a girl who once had gone with Cecil, but now was caught in the stronger of Lee's own two hands.

She was wearing a perfume, no doubt about it, the scent of it mixing with yet other good smells, that of starch, for example, and pastel clothes washed in Clorox and suds. Lee reeled. Her body was of just the right composition, which is to say quite firm and yet willing to go in any direction he wished. For him there was nothing in this world like female flesh.

"You sure do dance good," he said, drawing her closer.

"Hey!"

He drew back an inch or two. Her dress was of a pale blue, and she wore a brooch in the shape of a butterfly and yet, deep within, he knew that she was *not* the one who someday would be his wife. Meantime the song, his all-time favorite, was coming down to its conclusion just as he had always known that it would. Suddenly he began humming along with Billy Eckstine, causing her to pull back even further from his person.

It was dim inside the house, but still broad daylight without, and Lee, who never could be *completely* happy unless it were raining in the night, could feel himself falling into one of his moods. The music was ending, indeed *had* ended, and it was clear to him that this particular girl had no wish to stay out on the floor with him once the song was over. He let her go. He was not like Cecil, not yet, and very likely never would be.

His depression lasted only long enough for the beautiful "Tennessee Waltz" to come on. This great song, one of his favorites, alluded to an even finer piece of music that he had never actually heard. A gracious place, Tennessee, full of girls sitting about in lovely dresses having tea. He looked for a partner, finding her in the shape of a sixth-grader who appeared to be a little bit intimidated by the music and the dimness.

"Hi! Want to dance?" he asked, towing her out onto the floor. Having never viewed her up close before, her face was not exactly what he had supposed. Half-shielded in ambient shadows, he could see into but one of her eyes, a brown organ, highly dilated, full of rods and cones. He had chosen well, as he now conceded—she was prettier than he had attributed to her.

"I'm one of Cecil Price's friends," he said.

"I know."

Far away, Reese had now gotten into a fight with a boy from another town. He simply couldn't understand it, how anyone would wish to go up against Reese, far less someone from another town. Everyone feared Reese, but even Reese feared Cecil Price.

His sixth-grader didn't know how to dance. Shielding her from view, Lee made a few swaying movements intended to persuade anyone who might be watching that she *did* know how so to do.

"Cecil and me, we do all kinds of things."

"Yes, and you're going to get in trouble someday, too." And then: "What kind of things?"

But Lee wasn't taking any more questions. Instead, he shook his head sadly and looked off into the distance. Crime lay in his future, he was sure of it, and a short, tragic life.

"Anyway, it dudn't matter anymore."

"How come?"

"Be dead long before that day comes around."

The music was ending. Two of the boys were playing pool, an activity that Lee could never understand when one just as easily could be dancing. The cake, too, was less than half finished, and some three or four people, having clustered around it, were being served by the maid, a sweet woman, comely but black. Her hips were excessively large, however. Having carried the sixth-grader back to her station, Lee waited for the music. He had hoped they might replay some of the same songs, but was just as glad when instead they put on "Now and Then There's a Fool Such as I," an old-time classic that made him lean up against a nearby column for support. It was the beauty of things, of music, darkness, and the world. Panicked by it, he scanned the room for a girl, settling upon a nearby neighbor of his with whom he had never danced before.

"Hi!" he said. "Want to dance?"

She was strong, and he proved unable to actually bring
her out of the clot of girls giggling in the corner. One of
them wore a purple dress—his favorite color—but lacked
the sort of face that might have drawn him to her. His future wife, was *she* lurking among that crowd? No, probably not. No, he still expected to find her in France or
something like that.

And so thus Lee—he had thought all the best music
had been played already when that moment, he heard the
opening verse of "Everything I Have is Yours," adult music,
as he thought of it, which bore the most embarrassing and
tantalizing title he had ever heard. In his desperation he
headed for Mildred Weston, whose scholarly nature and
good grades now fell away into absolute unimportance.

"Hi," he said.

"I'm busy."

She was not busy. Lee then turned back to Brenda, who
had been doing a great part of the giggling. Truth was, he
had pretty well satisfied himself with this person during
their earlier associations, and he had far preferred to
dance with Preston's sister, a college-aged girl supervising
the music. Taking his courage, Lee went to her.

"Hi."

"Well hello." (Her voice was like an adult's.)

"Want to dance?"

She laughed. She was dressed in make-up, lipstick included, and had the sort of shiny legs that said she was
wearing hose. He felt foolish, Lee did, but considered it far
too late now to turn and go away.

"Alright."

He was dismayed. Was he supposed to put his hand on
her shoulder, which was largely exposed and no doubt
had been touched by football players and others? Instead
he coughed, once, politely, and then sought for her hand.
The music was ninety percent over and there was nothing
to be done until the next song. Meantime he was being

watched by Preston's mother, not to mention some fifteen or twenty boys and girls, all of them grinning in the patronizing way that Lee most loathed.

"Are you enjoying the party?" (Already she was bored with him. How to interest a nineteen-year-old—it was a problem.)

"Sure!" And then: "How about you?"

"Did you get enough cake?"

Cake! He had not come to this place for cake.

"I didn't come here for the cake."

The girl took two steps back and laughed out loud at him. He was about ready to abandon her there and never come back again when, that instant, the incredible "Till I Waltz Again with You" came on, blowing his resolution all apart. Now, slowly, he lifted his right hand and set it on the shoulder, partly exposed, of a nineteen-year-old girl. He swooned, his head grew dizzy, and his eyes, both of them, fell out of focus and began to spin. He must tell Cecil about this, this and his overall record with older girls. But no, it was private.

He had further pieces of good fortune on that day when the music began playing "Ebb Tide" and "Harbor Lights" and then, finally, "My Heart Cries for You," a song he had taken for his own personal theme. "Absolute scoundrel," the school principal had called him more than once, and it was true that after two hours of this sort of stuff he was on the verge of disgracing himself in plain open view over an aesthetic breakdown having to do with perfume and girls, darkness and music. That was when the lights came back on.

Lee groaned; in place of music, the time had come to take photographs of the dog. Lee, who had seen better animals wandering at large about the town, went and, inserting the four fingers of his right hand, Napoleon fashion, into his jacket, stood next to the creature while the man dithered with his camera. He estimated it at about

four in the afternoon, giving him but little time before
some of his better radio programs would come on. He was
also aware of several other things—that the girls, born to
pose, were cooing over the dog and, secondarily, that the
maid was cutting up the cake into great big pieces and
wrapping them in foil.

"Would y'all like to see our new television?" the woman
asked, addressing the group at large.

Silence. Some had heard of this new discovery, and
some had not. Even so, they followed into the next room
and collected around what might almost have been an
electrical washing machine, judging by the circular window of about the size of a dinner plate. He did not, Lee,
really expect any result from it, and could feel a certain
low-level exasperation while the husband and wife both
got down in front of the thing and began fuddling with
the little knobs that had something to do with it.

"It's a television," someone whispered.

"I know what it is! You don't have to tell me what it is."

Reese spoke up: "Maybe it's broken."

"You have to wait," said Lee to the girl next to him, a
tall person he had never seen before. "Wait for it to warm
up."

"Oh."

"It's not like a radio. It's different."

The girl turned and looked at him with respect. Already they were beginning to perceive the faint, far-away
sound of human voices, haunted noises coming from a
cave or cavern, one might almost have thought. No one
knew the depth and reach of the tubes and cables that
attached this machine to the outside world.

"Alright, here it comes! See?"

They gathered around as vague forms that looked like
photographic negatives began to manifest themselves in
front of their eyes.

"Hey! It's a wrestling match!"

"We know what it is. Just shut up, okay?"

The images were inside the box. As familiar as he was with his father's motion picture projector, he had a pretty good idea of the ingenuity of the thing.

"Aw, it's just a trick," Reese said.

"No, there's a projector in there."

"What did he say?"

"Projector."

"Interesting, interesting. No, I guess that's just about the stupidest thing I ever heard in my life."

Lee could feel his gorge rising. The tall girl had mean-time moved around to the other side, where he could no longer talk to her. That was when the negress came and handed off a good pound or more of vanilla cake wrapped in foil. Looking forward a few minutes into time, he could foresee himself carrying it home to his people.

Five

The next he knew, dawn had arrived, bringing morning with it. But as to how he had managed to get through the foregoing black night, he couldn't recall. Abandoning the bed with great reluctance, he gathered the tacks that he had set up in the doorway and returned them to the box. The smell that came from the kitchen was an alloy of bacon and grits and, no doubt, eggs as well. Coffee, too, though he wouldn't be allowed any. "Ah, me," said he, yawning and stretching and getting into his knickers. "Late September it is, and this person here"—he touched his face—"it feels like me."

In previous years, autumn had been better than this. But he had no reason to complain. The leaves, those that remained, were vibrating more and more fervidly as they turned to deeper and deeper grades of gold. He stopped and smote himself on the forehead—October it was and no longer September, to reckon from the days that had passed since the last time he had smoted himself there. He must cherish these days and store them up in memory against the decades yet to come. Far away he heard a dog screaming from the hills, the sound of bells, and neighborhood women gathering jars of unhomogenized milk brought to their front porches. Ten thousand years might go by, and still there'd be home deliveries of milk and doctors making house calls—such was Leland's naïveté at that particular time.

Nothing surprised him anymore, as he liked to think, and yet he was surprised, and greatly, to see Dexter waiting for him at the corner, the last thing Lee would have expected of October. Jumping into his bored expression, Lee moved forward, neither increasing his gait nor slowing it, either.

"Where you headed? Piss ass."

Lee pointed. "School."

"And what you got in that little bag there? I don't like that."

"Sandwich."

"What kind of sandwich! How many times I got to ask?"

"Pineapple." He looked off into the distance. Someday, when he was dead and gone, he expected to wander among mountaintops like those, where the atmosphere was blue and thin.

"Pineapple my ass! I already told you about this once! Ham and cheese is what I like, stuff like that."

"I know."

"Well, I guess I'm just going to have to beat the shit out of you. I don't *want* to do it, but I guess I got to."

Lee turned to the street. It was not impossible that one of the passing cars might have an adult in it who knew about him, and about Dexter. That was when a new concept came to mind, a stratagem that he hadn't used before. Clearing his throat, he spoke out loud and clear: "I'm one of Cecil Price's friends."

The boy's face took on a pinched look. "No, you ain't."

"I am too! So go ahead! Go ahead and beat the shit out of me!"

"I bet you don't even know Cecil."

"So go ahead and beat the shit out of me then! I want you to!"

"Naw, I don't want to hurt you."

"Go ahead!"

But Dexter had no more to say, and the last Lee saw of him he had turned and was trodding off in the other direction.

He, Lee, arrived at school in time and went and stood in the center of the grounds, a good location whence he could see everything that happened. He saw, for instance, a knot of girls whispering together excitedly about their trivia and then, further, his friend Cecil and his friend's friend, the girl named Gwen. Today her sweater was red, a hue that sorted perfectly with the vivid personality that was hers. If *he* had a woman like that—but he hadn't—he would have taken her out of general sight and kissed her on the mouth. But he didn't. And then, too, some of the older boys were playing baseball in a corner of the field. And now, once again, he began to feel that these matters had taken place ten thousand years ago and that he was looking out upon the world through a pane of glass. Would he never be free of this? Worst of all was the absolute silence that had come over the scene. Too late, he realized that Craig was nudging at his elbow.

They climbed the stairs together, both boys taking care not to collide into anyone from the upper classes. He regretted this wastage of the October weather, best time in the world for fishing and kites. "Ah, me," said he, lumping forward with his clarinet and sandwich. "I'd rather be free *now*, this very moment, and then make up for it later on."

Today, the class discussion centered upon the Babylonians. He personally knew of any number of places about
town where he could have picked up a calendar for free;
why, then, was the woman so full of praise for the Babylo-
nian one? In any case, he far preferred the Egyptians and
their ways. Getting into a thoughtful expression (eyes
closed), he began to tilt off to sleep, but only to be inter-
rupted by the start of one of his three-day headaches, a
routine affliction that had something to do with the person he was. Would only he could come back later on, snip
out these next few days, and splice the rest back together
once again! Something was wrong with him, of course, he
knew that and was aware, too, of the discontinuity between the activity in his head and his childlike behavior.
That was when a note came past, a brief one in yellow ink.
But he had rather die at once than break the moral code of
1950 and read as much as a single word of it.

He was largely unconscious when Cecil jostled him
awake, forced him to the outside world, and prodded him
forward toward the Teen Canteen.
   "S'matter?" the boy asked.
   "Nothing."
   "You're looking a little bit peaked today."
   "Naw."
   "Okay, you don't have to tell me if you don't want to."
   The place was dark, and they were playing one of the
earlier versions of "Ebb Tide," a song still much cherished
by Lee whether he had a headache or not. Six boys were
consuming Orange Drinks at the bar, one of them a football player surrounded by some half-dozen Corybantes in
shoes and socks. Striding forward confidently, Lee came to
within ten feet of that crowd before veering off toward his
wonted table in the corner. He had decided to keep away
from food, primarily because he had no funds. Cecil: "And
so you're just going to sit here. What, you been spending

your capital on *stamps* again?"

Lee admitted that he had. Not only had he invested his lunch money that way, but his thirty-five-cent a week allowance as well. Cecil went on: "Makes me mad! You need money, you're supposed to tell me about it."

"Okay, I will."

"No, you won't. I'll come back someday and you'll still be sitting right over here in this corner, getting smaller and smaller."

Lee had to laugh. He had a delicate temper, Cecil, but Leland was pretty sure he'd never use it against *him*. He was too small. And then, too, the jukebox had begun with "Now and Then There's a Fool Such as I," and Lee could feel himself falling back into the aesthetic trance that made him turn his head one way and another to look for girls. The place was dark, people were dancing, and the music was good. That was when Gwen, the loveliest girl in seventh grade, came and sat across from them. Never had he had seen her at such close range, and he was determined to get as good a picture of her as might be possible in the encompassing dim. Already their fingers were intertwined, hers and Cecil's, as Lee could plainly see by looking at them. Her sweater was fire green and had a piece of jewelry on it. As to how much further these two people were ready to go, Lee could only speculate. Suddenly she turned and smiled at Lee.

"It's all right, Lee. Because we're in love."

"Good Lord."

"It hurts, we're so much in love. I just can't hardly stand it anymore."

"Yeah. Cecil told me."

"What did he tell you?" (The question was directed at Lee, but the girl was watching Cecil.)

"Said you were in love."

"And did he say whether he loved *me*?"

"Sure!"

"What did he say?"

"Love."

They were looking deep into one another's eyes, those two, so much so that Lee felt he ought really to arise now and leave them to their project. The music meantime had rotated over once again to "Till I Waltz Again with You," Lee's seventh- or eighth-favorite piece at that particular time. Across the way, one of the boys was slapping at his pants, whereupon Lee now bent and examined his own cuff to be certain no one had deposited something there. There were at least five high school girls at the bar, including a certain Jenny Bird, a twelfth-grader who took lessons in ballet and was known to own a car. As for the girl who had forced a kiss upon him, Lee found her nowhere, neither on the floor, nor at the counter, nor in the green room where now and again he could see figures dancing in the gloom. Cecil meantime had joined up his spare hand with Gwen's, and it seemed to Lee that probably they were playing with each other's feet beneath the table. How, really, did it feel to be like that, in love in 1950? He knew this much, Lee, that it was a new romantic age in the history of the world, and never mind how brief.

Meantime the music had gone over to "Harbor Lights," making it impossible for Cecil and Gwen to resist going to the floor to dance. Lee watched studiously as the boy brought her up close and gazed down unsmilingly into her eyes. Such was the music, it seemed that some of the couples had actually fallen to sleep in one another's arms. It was a serious and private business, and, really, a person ought not be watching. Working hurriedly, he finished off his Orange Drink and was in the process of getting to his feet when he experienced a hand on his shoulder, the hand of an adult, as it seemed to him.

"Leland?"

"Sir?"

It *was* an adult.

"If you'll just step outside, please. If you're not too busy, that is."

"Okay."

He rose—people were watching—and followed the man through the dark. He could almost certainly have outrun this person, but was unwilling to do so owing to the indignity it would have involved. Instead, putting on a bored face, he stepped out into the painful light of the Sun and turned to face the individual whom he had seen once or twice before when he had also been in trouble.

"Is this how you spend your time, Leland? Over here with these people?"

"Yes, sir."

"You're supposed to be in the cafeteria! Just like everybody else."

"Yeah, but . . ."

"What?"

"I don't like those pimento cheese sandwiches all the time."

"Anybody else in there?"

"No, sir. Some high school kids."

"I'm not talking about them! I'm talking about *junior* high people."

"No, sir."

"Smitty's not in there?"

"No, sir!"

"Cecil?"

"Who?"

"Cecil Price!"

Lee thought. "I know a guy named Pratt."

"Well, I guess you better come with me. Mr. Debarbeleben's going to want to talk to you."

"Yes, sir. Maybe I could talk to him later."

"You'll talk to him right now, is what you'll do!"

It was not the first time Lee had seen these precincts. The same woman sat at the typewriter, a motherly sort of person who smiled sympathetically as Lee strode past with his reckless and nihilistic air. He had promised himself *not* to urinate on this occasion, no matter how many blows he was to be given or which of his many paddles the man might opt to use. There was a portrait of General Hood on the facing wall, and Lee was able to concentrate upon that man's life and activities, and in that way fortify himself against the ordeal still to come. Thus passed two minutes, Lee making no comment to the boy sitting next to him.

"What are you in for?" he courteously inquired at last.

"Smoking."

"Whew!"

"You?"

"Canteen."

"Oh, shit."

"But I was only there a little while!"

"That don't matter. I know a fellow who . . ."

Lee waved it away. He didn't wish to hear about these fellows who in some cases had already taken thirty or forty blows in the course of September alone.

". . . got more than a hundred last year."

"Oh, God."

"It's getting worse. And he's getting meaner all the time."

"I know."

"I don't know if I can take any more myself."

"How many have *you* had?"

"Fifteen. And this is just October."

"Oh, God."

"But he might go easy on you. 'Cause you're so little and everything."

"I *am* small," Lee admitted. "But my grades are pretty good."

"That won't do you no good. How old are you?"

"Eleven."

"Eleven, shit! I'm fourteen myself."

Lee was not surprised, certainly not in view of the boy's incipient moustache.

"Well," Lee said, stretching and making his face more bored even than before, "*I'll* never see fourteen, that's for sure."

"How come?"

"Liver. It's no good."

"Well, I'm real sorry to hear it." (The boy had red hair and a medley of giant freckles as big as dimes.)

"Nobody knows, except you. I just don't want people *worrying* about me too much."

"Right."

They turned and, after examining each other for the underlying integrity, shook with solemnity. They were just getting to know each other, Lee felt, when the woman came and, smiling sweetly, invited the older boy into the office. He believed, Lee, that he still had a good ten or fifteen minutes before his own appointment, and almost jumped out of his skin when, that moment, the boy began shrieking in the next room. Apparently the man was in an exasperated mood, the worst of all possible eventualities at that particular time.

"Good Lord!" said Leland to himself. He had counted four blows, and with no suggestion that they might be coming to an end. Near to urinating, he looked for support to General Hood and the crippled arm bound to his side. It was astonishing how the woman kept on typing, adjusting her rhythm to the flagellation going on just twenty feet away. They looked at each other, the typist and Lee.

"You see, Lee, what happens?"

"Yes, ma'am."

"So let it be a lesson to you."

"Yes, ma'am. I do."

"I know how disappointed your father is going to be."

Lee also knew.

"And I have to put it in your record, too." She nodded

toward the document, an extensive page with a good deal
of inscription on it already. Lee waved it away. It wasn't
the paper he dreaded nearly so much as the superintendent's strong right arm. Came then the fifth shriek, assuming Lee had counted rightly. His last best hope—and
Leland had never understood how a last hope could fail to
be the best—his last hope was that the man would have
exhausted himself by now and his anger been somewhat
abated. That was when his new-made friend spurted out
of the office and ran off down the hall, holding his but-
tocks in one hand.

"Next!" the man called.

Lee stood and, grinning appealingly at the woman,
pulled open the door. He needed a moment for his eyes to
adjust to the prevailing dimness of that place, a capacious
area with a desk and a range of bookshelves that reached,
almost, to the ceiling. The man himself stood in the center, his sleeves rolled to the elbows.

"So," he said. "We meet again."

"Yes, sir. I guess."

"Now what do we have on schedule for you today, Lee?
Two hundred licks?"

His knees weakened and he reached out, Leland, to
catch hold of a piece of furniture; two hundred was death;
he knew it, and the man knew it, too.

"All I did was go over to the Canteen! And I didn't do
anything, either!"

"You fixing to cry, Lee? I'm surprised at you."

"No, sir." (He was *not* going to cry, not now and not
ever.) And then: "I'm one of Cecil Price's friends."

"No doubt. And I suppose he was over there too, yes?"

Lee, declining to answer, looked for and discovered a
massy armchair facing the man's official desk.

"Did I say you could sit down? Odd. I don't remember
that."

Lee jumped up. The man had a circular face, much

weathered, and his nostrils, two matched holes, gave his appearance the look of an electrical outlet. Taking himself by the lapels, he now strode over to his famous "cabinet," so-called, and drew out a paddle of about three feet in length with three holes bored in it for blisters. The thing was thin and flexible, and had been varnished to match his desk.

"This is what I use on Smitty and Charlie T., people like that. And Cecil."

"Charlie T. and Smitty are the same people."

"Oh?" His face took on a puzzled look. The paddle was more flexible than he knew, so much so that he could bend it back "upon itself," so to speak. "See this? How it bends back and forth?"

Having declined to cry, Lee looked out over the yard where in former days he had been wont to run his heedless ways. There was a dog out there, also the figure of Clarence, who had been expelled last year and didn't know what to do with himself. Meantime the man had gone to his closet and had exchanged his three-foot paddle for something shorter and with only one hole in it.

"Bend over. Grab your ankles."

Lee bent. It was a humiliating posture, not something he would have wanted a girl to see. The first blow would tell whether he could endure those to follow. He had decided to think of his rear end as actually belonging to someone else.

Truth was, he *heard* the noise before he experienced the effect. "And so sound really does travel faster than nerves," he said. "Interesting." Came then the effect.

"Whew!" he said, straightening and hopping about in a circle. "I didn't think it would be like that!"

"No? What *did* you think?"

"I thought you'd just give me a warning, maybe."

"Would it do any good? Bend over, Lee. Don't make me mad."

Lee held his breath, but the results were just the same.

"Good Lord! Say, how come you have to hit *so hard*?"

"Listen, my boy, I spent *three years* in teachers' college learning how to do this. Come on, bend over, don't make me mad."

The third blow was not so awful. The man was tiring, either that or Lee had become hardened to it over the course of the past half-minute. At this rate, the two hundredth blow would be as nothing.

"What are you reading these days, Lee?"

"Sir?"

"Reading."

"Well, I'm reading this one book about a guy that lived on an island all by himself, and he . . ."

"Okay, that's all right. What else?"

"Well, I'm reading a book about this other guy who used to hunt tigers, and he . . ."

"That's a child's book, Lee. You can do better than that."

"It's good!"

"No, it's not. We have a library in this very building, my friend, with far better stuff than that."

He had a headache, Lee, his gorge was rising, *and* his left buttock was largely paralyzed. The man went on: "And how is it, my friend, that you do Cecil's homework for him and yet he makes better grades than you? Is it pride, Lee? No, I'd really like to know."

"He would take his girlfriend with him, and one day she killed the biggest tiger of all."

"Yes, but we're not talking about that anymore."

"No, sir."

"You're so lucky, and you don't even know it. Look around you, Lee; it's 1950."

Lee looked. Off in the distance, he saw Preston on his bicycle. The boy had been scheduled for a series of dental appointments and was required twice a month to go downtown for that reason. Further, Lee saw the smoke-stack of the county's primary employer, a thirty-acre waste littered with rusting equipment where automobile engine manifolds were built.

"But are you listening? It has one hundred fifty million well-matched people, this country of ours, and the level of prosperity is just exactly right. One dollar more would be too much. And Lee?"

"Sir?"

"Every time I hear the word 'progress,' that's when I draw my revolver."

Always, Leland had regarded this person with respect, and not merely on account of his strong right arm. He watched with fascination as the man now returned to his bureau and took out a broad-brim hat made of felt and put it on.

"This here is my *prophesying* hat, Lee, my wife calls it."

"Yes, sir. Reese told me about it."

"It lets me see into the future. Greatest thing since the invention of shoes and socks." And then: "Ha! You thought I was going to say since the 'wheel,' didn't you? Hey! Did I say you could sit?"

Lee jumped up. "Shoes, yes, sir. Shoot, I reckon they're just about the most important thing there is."

"Don't patronize me, boy. I haven't forgotten why you're here."

"No, sir."

"Bad things, that's what I see. A land of four hundred million odd-matched people living tentative lives. By then, you see, America will have become the name of an economy only, and no longer a country."

"Nothing surprises me, not anymore."

"Negroes, Lee—I see absolute negroes sitting in the halls of Congress."

Lee laughed.

"And women. Let me ask you, Lee—who makes the decisions in *your* house? Your mommy or your daddy?"

"Daddy."

"See?"

"But she makes dinner."

"Fair enough. Remember this, Lee: the primacy *always* belongs to men. Just imagine if it were the other way around."

Lee wrote it down in memory. The following blow had no real force behind it, none to speak of, and Lee began to believe that he might actually escape the remaining 196. It also encouraged him to see that the man had taken off his hat and had put it away among the paddles.

"Remember!"

Outside, he hobbled back to the main building and was about to collect his clarinet when Cecil stopped him.

"How many did he give you?"

Lee looked down.

"Bastard! Was it fifteen?"

He nodded in the negative, Lee.

"Son-of-a-bitch! He tried that on Clarence last year."

"Yeah," spoke up Charlie T. "But ole Clarence beat the shit out of him."

"I have a headache, too," said Lee, pointing to his liver.

To relieve him of the weight, Cecil took his clarinet and then guided him down the hall toward where the band was waiting. Six majorettes in short pants were posing for photographs at the back of the room where the trumpet players were facing off in different directions, each playing his own music, as it were. Meantime the saxophonist, a quondam friend, was sitting in the corner, playing the Tony Bennett version of "Because of You." Feeling that he was home again and safe, Lee glanced about at the group, pleased to see how well the musicians matched their instruments, a ratio in which the most outstanding boys played the shiniest horns. They had three minutes and no more before the conductor would make his appearance and force the lot of them into one organized song. Instead—and he hated these interludes—strangeness gradually fell down over him, and once again he began to feel that he was far away, able to see but not to hear, a crowd of puppets going through their motions.

He walked home that afternoon in the gathering gloom. The days were growing shorter, no question about it. Furthermore, the economy had begun to sputter, President Truman's fault, according to the adults. Moving through the bad district, he saw a small, naked boy standing out in a yard and then, next, a disabled car that hadn't been there six hours earlier. He glanced at his watch. He had set the thing ahead to New York time, but it had run down again, and he had only a short while to get him to his radio, his milk and wafers, and today's *Sky King*. In spite of that, he stopped and waited for his brother to turn the corner three blocks back and make an inch-tall appearance against the sky. Mrs. Findlay's plum tree was nearly bare—October it was—and he had no wish to appropriate the few fruits that still adhered to the upper branches. He still did have his headache, of course, and would need another full day before it would go away.

He slept that night between patterned sheets, and then woke to the realization that he had just been through a dream of such great filthiness that he would never wish to discuss it further. Meantime the dog had taken a tack in his paw, and it needed Lee several minutes and his flashlight to draw it out. It was true that he had lately acquired some twenty pieces of pre-war Hungarian postage, using most of his lunch money on them, and they were crying out, so to speak, to be put away in the album. Outside, a car went by, Mr. Kaiser's 1948 Frasier or, possibly, Mr. Frasier's 1948 Kaiser—he wasn't sure. In any case, the headlights penetrated the curtains and sent horrible silhouettes bounding across the ceiling and walls. Too chilly to go outside, Lee opted to read, choosing for that purpose a boring book that he thought the school principal might approve. Two pages of it and he resorted to the window, whence he could observe that the Moon was afflicted with many more black spots than just the night before. The Age of Man was ending. As to the clouds, they had taken on the shapes of some of the ink blots that had been used to test him. He saw bats running behind the Moon, and then an airship in full sail, with pennants furling from the masts. "Good Lord," he said. "I must be asleep after all!" And was.

Six

He awoke as usual and then, to minimize the time that he needed to be naked, an immoral condition in his opinion, scurried from his pajamas into his jeans. It promised to be a remarkable day, even if he couldn't right away remember why. Accordingly, he finished off his breakfast in prompt style and, after checking in the mirror to see if he still produced a reflection, ran off down the sidewalk with his pencil box and pineapple sandwich. He allowed three minutes for Sonya to come along, and when she failed to do so, waited half a minute more for Linda, who failed also. Resigned to it, he walked with Mildred Weston. All his life he had known that a boy must walk *between* a girl and the traffic, fencing her off from danger. But with her he had to fight for it.

"Hey," he said, "*I'm* supposed to walk here. Not you."

"Oh, for goodness sakes."

She gave way to him, however, and for a full block, no other word was said, until: "I've been doing lots of reading lately. Books."

"I doubt it."

"Mr. Debardeleben wants me to."

"That's not what I heard."

"Hm?"

"Twenty-five licks—*that's* what *I* heard."

"Yes, and I had a headache, too."

Useless. A thousand years might go by before he'd win any respect from this person who, in any case, was perhaps the fourth- or fifth-least-lovely girl anywhere. Even so, he stayed with her for another moment or two before abandoning her to his brother, who was moving up quickly from behind.

It was when he came within sight of the schoolyard that he recollected why this day was sure to prove so memorable: A chartered bus, fifty feet long, was parked in the yard. Lee ran forward, first to collect his clarinet and then, secondarily, to join with Cecil and the others waiting to climb on board. Gwen, too, was there, but not because she was in the band. No, she had come to say farewell to Cecil, whom she wouldn't see again for the rest of that day. Lee came closer, listening to her.

"Oh, God, I can't stand it."

"You got to," Cecil said, his voice strained. "Anyway, I'll be back tonight."

"Oh, God. It's so *mean*, making you go away like this!"

"I got no choice. Anyway, I'm coming back."

They embraced, Lee coming nearer. Her hair was blonde, and her lips were decorated with a bright lipstick that matched her character and very red sweater. Looking her up and down, Lee could verify the on-going development of her withers and brisket, already so much like an adult's. What was it like, to hold a creature like that in one's own arms? He shivered, Lee, and then went around to the other side, where Lloyd and Craig were striving to disentangle their saxophones from the immense pile of instruments that lay in the yard. Three majorettes in short pants were approaching from the distance, followed by two trombonists and the town's leading percussionist. Just then an automobile, a black Packard, drove out onto the field itself and came toward them. Lee quickly put on a serious expression and stood at attention while the conductor climbed slowly from his car and scanned the crowd.

"All right, gentlemen. Ladies. Smitty. Gather 'round!"

They gathered. He was a vulpine man with thinning hair, deep-set eyes, and a voice damaged by laryngitis. Lee feared him, he admitted it, fearing him more, with some dozen exceptions, than anyone on Earth.

"Yes," the man went on, "today we go to Tuscaloosa. And if we don't come back with the blue ribbon, so much the worse for you! No, this is serious business. You hear me, Preston?"

"Yes, sir."

"Serious! And I expect *every one of you*, Cecil, to do the best playing you can. No, wait a minute, that won't be good enough. I expect you to do *better* than you can, right? And if you think you're going to go barging into this nice little town they got down there and steal everything in sight . . . Well, you can just forget about that, Reese."

"Yes, sir."

"Don't even *think* about doing any stealing. I haven't forgotten last year, not by a long shot. You read me?"

They all said, "Yes, sir."

"No stealing. But if you just got to steal something, for God's sakes, don't get caught!"

They now filed on board the bus, the most crucial moment of that particular year. Depending on it, a person could end up sitting next to his choice of persons, or not. But mostly Lee was impressed by the luxuriousness of the conveyance, the upholstered seats, the low ceiling, and sheltered ambiance that cut them off from adult surveillance, save only that of one. And even that person had chosen to sit near the front.

Lee hastened to the rear of the bus and claimed the

seat next to the window of the next-to-last berth. It was possible that one of the majorettes in short pants might elect to join him here, though he didn't really expect that. He would have welcomed a woodwind or flautist almost as much, but was even more pleased when he saw there were enough seats for everyone, and he was to have a whole berth for himself alone. Two trumpet players had meanwhile taken up just across from him, and as he looked about, Lee recognized that all the more vivid personalities had chosen this part of the bus. He could not have been more pleased. He turned to speak to Cecil, but then, suddenly, jumped back, startled to see that Gwen was coming with them after all.

"Hey!" he said. "*You* aren't in the band."

"Just shut up, okay?" Cecil said.

Stunned with admiration, Lee agreed to say no more.

They drove to the outskirts of town and proceeded down a narrow street lined on both sides with grocery stores, gas stations, and negro shacks with people sitting on the porches. They passed a church without windows, inside it a crowd of negroes singing hymns. It is true that most of the garbage cans were upright, though only by a thin majority. A dog (dog with mange) walked past, wearing a haughty expression. He would have cured that dog, Lee, had the dog been his, yea, and would have righted the garbage cans as well. Continuing with his observations, he saw a dead chicken rotting on a roof and then, next, a fat woman too drugged fully to lift her feet off the ground. However, so long as these people *stayed within their own neighborhoods,* Lee had no grudge against them.

By 9:30 they had broken out of the city altogether and were sailing through a brown and umber countryside characteristic of November in 1950. These were historic lands, these, where not so long before red Indians would have been seen traveling back and forth. Today he was rejoiced by barns and scuppernong arbors, a worn-out

mule pressing at the fence, a piece of abandoned machin-
ery where twenty years ago someone had run off and left
it, and then, finally, best of all, a farmer's wife who had
come down to the highway to look into her mailbox. This
woman might almost have been his own grandmother,
except that in place of a calico bonnet she had opted for
gingham blue. How many children had she not raised,
how many cows and vegetable gardens, and would ever
she be given credit for it by the big city commentators
who cared nothing for such things?

She would not, and when they came to the top of the
next hill, Lee's attention was taken by Cecil and Gwen so
entangled in the back seat that they were beginning to
look like one person. It is true that it was dim aboard the
bus, that the windows were tinted, and that someone had
brought along a radio now playing "Now and Then There's
a Fool Such as I." It was private, this thing that Cecil and
Gwen were doing, but as one of that person's best friends,
Lee felt he was entitled to turn from time to time and
monitor what was going on. He had not seen smooching
on this scale in a long time; never, in fact, and it interested
him to see how it was done.

"Hey!"

"Naw, I'm just looking."

"Well, get your own girl!"

"Where?"

Cecil indicated about with his free arm, a gesture that
seemed to encompass the whole bus. "Linda."

"Naw, she doesn't even like me anymore."

Nevertheless, Lee stood and scanned the seats. She *was*
there, the girl called Linda, but she sat near the front of
the bus where there was too much light and where the
band director was reading in a publication of some kind.
Even so, he went forward and took up the place just behind her.

"Hi!" he said.

"No, no, and no!"

Lee went back. There were at least four other persons (other than Cecil and Gwen) seated behind him on the back bench, and one of these was an eighth-grade girl, assuming he remembered correctly from the last time he had seen her. Yawning and putting on a bored expression, he turned fully around and tried to discern her in the dark.

"Hi."

She smiled. It was dark back there, especially in the corners, and he could see only the least part of her face and the contours of her bell-shaped head.

"Boy howdy," he said, nodding toward Cecil. "They sure are smooching over there."

She laughed. "Well, don't look at them, then."

"It's private?"

"Yes!"

"Oh."

Nothing more to be said, Lee turned again and faced forward. It surprised him to see that Michael, previously a shy person, had seated himself next to the xylophonist and had his arm about her shoulders. But were these two truly congruent with each other? Meantime the music had rotated over to the beautiful "Tennessee Waltz," and once again Lee could feel himself succumbing to the magic of that particular voice. They, however, were running to the *South*, further from Tennessee and toward New Orleans. Suddenly, just then, the noise of thunder broke out overhead, bringing with it the promise of dimness abetted by opaque rains.

Could anything be more welcome than this? No, and when he thought about it, looking back over the waste of years, it came to him that all the best things that had come to him, when they came, came in spates and spades. He shivered violently, largely because a new thought had just now come into mind, namely that they were running, not simply through countryside but time as well, and that in days to come no one would be left alive to remember any of it. Could anything be less welcome than that? To have been given the half-life of a molecule ricocheting among girls? He took out a stick of gum that bore a substance on it designed to calm his nerves. Of rains, he gave this one a "six" on his ten-scale. It was dense enough to make a noise on the roof, and fluid enough to drain off down the windowpanes; it was not, however, remotely like those Old Testament deluges of his desire. Hewing to the window, he observed a field full of smiling cows exulting in the stuff. Those barns and farmhouses, were their roofs in good repair? Suddenly, just then, a bolt of jagged lightning plunged to earth and lodged there in an upright position for what to Lee seemed a very long time.

Toward the front, someone was practicing on an English Horn, a mellow sound that sorted so well with the rain that it saddened Lee to think that it must end someday. He turned to speak with Cecil, but then turned back again when he saw the boy was engaged. At this rate the boy and girl would be married, figuratively speaking, before they came to Tuscaloosa. Thinking of it, Lee then turned again and, in spite of things, spoke up in a soft but still audible voice: "Cecil?"

"Yeah."

"What y'all going to do when we get there?"

"I don't know. What, you getting nervous again?"

"No! Shoot, no. Maybe we could get something to eat."

The boy said nothing. He had gotten his left arm about the girl's neck and, although she didn't seem to mind, had forced her face into a "star-gazing" position, as it were. Lee came closer, observing how he kissed her about the nose and eyes, and then the lips themselves.

"We could go to a restaurant. Get a cheeseburger."

"Right."

"So I guess I'll just link up with you and Gwen then."

"Figured you would." (His right hand reached toward the girl's sweater, but then drew back just in time.)

"Maybe an Orange Drink, too."

"Sloan?"

"Yes?"

"Shut-up, okay?"

"Yeah, I think I'll just . . ." He turned around. He had by no means forgotten the eighth-grade girl, who continued to sit prudentially in the extreme corner of the bus where the rain was heaviest and had set up a veil of sound, so to describe it, between himself and the person. Thinking of her, he waited five seconds before again turning about in his seat and, shielding his eyes, searching for her in the dark.

"Boy howdy," he said, "it sure is coming down out there."

She smiled. Half an hour had gone by, and he knew no more about her than if they had not both been woodwind players.

"The rain," I mean.

"Yes."

"Lightning, too."

"I know."

Lee nodded. So far they were in agreement about everything.

"I guess you're in the eighth grade, probably."

"I used to be. But I'm in the ninth grade now."

Lee reeled. He had seen it before, this abnormal appeal that older women exercised upon him. He stretched lazily and putting on a bored expression, said, "I have a lot of respect for ninth-graders. I guess I'll be there pretty soon myself."

She laughed out loud at him, a gesture that brought her face out into the light where he could see it. He had to admit that she was pretty, prettier even than he had construed from the sound of her voice. As for her hair, always one of his favorite substances, it was the color of chocolate and had a barrette in it. But what if he were to do to her what Cecil was doing? Meantime their two faces were only twelve to fourteen inches apart. And so of course that was when the radio, after a lengthy hiatus of advertisements, began playing the incredible Billy Eckstine version of "My Foolish Heart."

He couldn't stand it. Up front, Michael had left off with the xylophonist and was sitting next to Sonya Hunter. As for the conductor, he appeared to have gone to sleep, either that or he wanted to give his musicians their one good chance to behave as if they were no longer on school property. Smitty was smoking cigarettes. Lee's eye then traveled to the driver, a tired-looking individual who appeared wholly indifferent to the things going on in his mirror. Nothing was surprising anymore, and for him life had come to a stop many years ago. This conformed to Lee's general theory about the world—that it had a great deal more deterioration in it than the other way around.

They went on until just past ten, never stopping until the piccolo player, a girl not much smaller than Lee, went forward and whispered into the conductor's ear. Lee was not averse to a toilet break at this particular time, although it disappointed him that the girls, even the prettiest of them, were subject to the same imperatives as the males.

The rain was not as dense as before, and the boys, most of them, were able to dash quickly enough into the nearest trees. Craig meantime had headed off in the wrong direction but then soon turned around and came to the boys' side of the highway. He could urinate now, Lee, or continue on for another hundred miles—it didn't matter to him. Indeed, he enjoyed testing himself against these "requirements," so-called, that excited only his contempt. Far more important to him was it that his pencil box was getting wet. Nor was he much affected by the rain, a natural phenomenon, portending nothing, that he had witnessed ten thousand times before. Moving through the cows, a bored expression on his face, he joined up with Cecil and Holly Parker, peeing collaboratively on a disused ant hill. Gwen was not with them, Lee was pleased to see. In fact they could not be seen by any of the girls, nor could Lee see *them*, and finally gave up trying. Suddenly he jumped back, nonplussed to find that the band director had come with them and was peeing as well.

"Sir?" Lee said.

"Yes?" (He sounded impatient, though it was only just past ten o'clock.)

"My reed is broken."

"Don't tell me that."

"It is."

"Oh, boy. You've had *two months* to get ready for this!"

"Yeah, but . . ."

"Two months! What are you going to do, Lee, when you get to be a grown-up man? Go through life with a broken reed? That won't work!"

Lee looked down, declining to speak of the brevity of the life that he foresaw for himself. "Maybe I could just pretend to be playing."

"And why not? After all, that's more or less what you've been doing ever since I let you in the band."

"Yeah, but . . ."

"Borrow one from Craig."

Lee thought. It *was* possible that person might lend him one.

"What if he doesn't have an extra one?"

The man stopped, looked at him, and then tucked himself back in and zipped his fly. It was a new experience for Lee to witness an adult talking and urinating at the same time.

"Lee?"

"Sir?"

"What happened to you? Your father is a fine man, *real* fine."

"Yeah, but . . ."

"And just look at you standing over there. No reed, nothing."

A crow flew over, its voice as hoarse as the conductor's. Far away he thought that he could see some of the girls, much refreshed, squealing through the rain. They had come not even partway to Tuscaloosa and already the man was mad at him, his hair was wet, and he had lost account of the ninth-grade girl who used to sit behind him.

The next twenty-three miles were comparable, save only that they had turned off onto a tangential highway that was narrower but longer, and that on one occasion had them riding above the level of the encompassing trees. But Lee had been mistaken about the girl; fact is, she had returned to her place at the back of the bus and had positioned herself in darkness once again. Lee yawned and stretched, and after putting on a bored expression, glanced back to verify that it was she. As to Cecil, he had dropped off to sleep, as also the girl Gwen—they were in need of rest—reclining on his shoulder. Lee came nearer. He had suspected for some time that she wore a bit of make-up about her eyes, a habit that he was to discover more and more often among girls progressing from grade to grade.

What did they want, girls? Whatever it was, they wanted it badly. He understood, of course, why it was that boys liked girls, but was *never* to understand how it could be the other way around. As for the towns along the way, the local economies would have collapsed long before except for the beauty parlors and dress shops in these places. Coming closer, he was then able to descry at the juncture of Gwen's gingham sleeve what looked to him like the strap of a white brassiere. Why? She didn't need that, not at this stage. It seemed that she was impatient and wanted to be a full-blown woman *now*. Such was Leland's philosophy of women at that particular time.

The rain had come back again and the radio was playing one of the very best songs of that or any other decade. Without any decent sort of voice himself, Lee remained silent as the rest of the bus joined their voices with Patti Page's. It pleased him that Cherise, a restrained girl normally, was singing too, and that her face had taken on an appearance that was several degrees lovelier even than usual. Thousands of years might go by and still the song would be wending its way through space—Lee's philosophy at that time.

He slept briefly, but then was very rudely brought back to consciousness when he saw the rain had stopped. All his life it had been like this. Never would he understand it, how rains could be so short, days so long, and nights as hasty as they were. It was a long way to Tuscaloosa from his own hometown, and he had wanted to pass the whole of it in rain, darkness, music, and girls; instead, that moment, the bus began to sputter and then rolled to a stop.

"Cecil!" he called. "The bus!"

The boy immediately came awake, jumped up, and got into a defensive posture. He had forgotten, Lee, to rouse him by degrees.

"What?"

"Bus! We're stuck!"

Moving delicately, the boy lifted Gwendolyn's head and put it elsewhere. A commotion had broken out near the front, and in the mirror, Lee could see the driver wearing a peeved expression. It might not be a bad thing, Lee philosophized, to be fixed here for several days and nights with some of these people, a more pleasing future than having to get up on stage with a broken reed.

"Well," he said. "I guess we're stuck."

"Gosh, thanks for telling us, Lee," Mattie Lou remarked, her sole comment the whole journey. Lee then followed Cecil out into the rain and stood about as the boy clambered up under the bus, stayed a while, and then came back out again. He found himself, the clarinetist, standing among the bus driver, the band director, and Cecil. There was a problem here, and their faces reflected that.

"Blast it," the director was saying. "It never fails. Never!"

"Well, *he* ought to be able to fix it," Lee reported, pointing at the driver. "It's his job!"

"Shut up, Lee. What d'you think, Cecil?"

"I *might* be able to do it," the boy said. "If I had me a flashlight. And wrench."

"Heck, he could do it easily!" Lee said. "If he had a wrench."

"I get paid to *drive* this bus," the other man said. "I *don't* get paid to wallow around in the mud."

"And screwdriver."

"Or, if we could find a telephone somewhere."

"That won't do it. Need a wrench."

Four other boys had now departed from the vehicle, all wearing serious expressions. Lee's philosophy was verified—how that men are at their best when there's a job to be done. He would have gone under the bus himself, had only he but understood its workings.

"Maybe we could borrow one."

"Naw, there ain't any other buses around here."

Indeed, it was a long and level plain with only a very few farmhouses anywhere to be seen.

"Borrow a *wrench*, I'm talking."

"Yeah, but what about a flashlight? Good Lord, you can't expect him to do anything without a flashlight, for crying out loud."

"And nobody even mentions the screwdriver."

"Well. It's a mess, that's for sure."

The driver had gone back in, followed by two of the boys. Lee found himself standing about in company with the conductor, Cecil, two boys, and a girl. In just seven hours, the sky would begin to darken and night would be coming in. His shirt was full of mud, Cecil's, and he had taken on a certain soldierly aspect that Lee had seen in him so many times before, whether on the football field or dancing with girls in the Teen Canteen.

The Sun was weak and soon they would need flashlights just to find their ways in the dark. He, Lee, was about to go back in and reassure the girls; instead, that was when the bandleader came to his decision: "Okay, so be it; we need to ask these people"—he pointed off into the distance—"if we can borrow some tools."

Rather than venturing too far from the group, the same girl that only a moment ago had been peering beneath the bus now turned and reentered the vehicle where the seventh- and eighth-graders were singing a Nat Cole song. Already Cecil had begun to march toward the nearest farmhouse, an unpainted structure with an old-fashioned windmill bending to earth.

"Now Lee," the man went on, "I want you to volunteer to ask those people over there"—he pointed distantly toward a house with columns, a nineteenth-century plantation, as it almost seemed—"and ask those people for help. That will make up for a lot of things."

"Yes, sir. It's raining."

"I know it is. And that will make up for even more."

He set out, Leland, moving forward for some fifty yards before coming back and handing off his pencil box. There were at least fifteen faces looking out at him from the bus with various expressions of sympathy and contempt. A pretty good deal, it seemed to him, inasmuch as there seemed to be more sympathy than contempt. And then, too, he had some curiosity about the plantation, a place fit for a Nathan Bedford Forrest, he would have said, or a

Robert E. Lee.

Could anything be more inefficient than walking through rain? And if he wanted to be somewhere, why couldn't he get there through the workings of thought alone? Suddenly he stopped, pleased that the girl at the back of the bus was watching sadly as he disappeared into the distance. Putting on a tragic face, he slumped forward, indifferent to the condition of his shoes and socks and the rivulets running down his spine. All his life he had wanted to die by lightning strike, either that or in hand-to-hand combat with a crowd of Yankees.

The home, when he came to it, was not nearly as picture-worthy as he had thought. A child had left its toys out in the rain, including a clothen bear with a pained expression. Lee knocked twice, using his left hand at first and then the brass apparatus affixed to the door. From inside he heard the voice of Gabriel Heatter speaking over the radio, and then footsteps coming in his direction.

"Yes, ma'am," he said, putting on a sincere expression, "seems like our bus broke down and . . ."

"Why, you're soaked to the skin! Can't you see it's raining out there?"

She was a white woman with a maternal instinct, somewhere about forty or fifty years in age, judging from her neck and upper arms. She wore large fur slippers and had pretty clearly given up on her appearance. She had more immediate concerns, Lee supposed, and her husband and no longer noticed.

"Yes, ma'am. But he told me to come on over here."

"Well, shame on him. Is that your bus?"

"Yes, ma'am. Broken."

"I see! And who are all those people?"

"Just a bunch of kids. We're going to Tuscaloosa."

"Well, gracious. Maybe my husband could pull it out with our tractor."

"No, ma'am; it still wouldn't run. Anyway, Cecil can fix

it if he has a screwdriver. I'll bring it right back."

"My husband is pretty good at things like that."

"No, ma'am; Cecil can do it."

She left him at the door, just as he had known she would. It was dry inside and he saw a number of formal-looking portraits on the wall of stern-looking people in golden frames. A child sat crying on the staircase, and the kitchen had a negress in it. Feeling that he was getting bored, Lee stripped off his shirt and was wringing it out when the lady came back and offered him a selection of two screwdrivers, neither of them of entirely appropriate size. He mulled over the choice, finally settling on the newest one.

"We sure do appreciate it," he said, smiling endearingly.

"But don't you need an umbrella or something?"

"Yes, ma'am."

"Well, let me get you one!"

"No, ma'am. 'Cause then I'd have to bring it back."

"But you'd be dry, at least."

"No, ma'am. 'Cause then I'd just have to go back again without any umbrella."

There was some sense in that, as at last she seemed to understand.

"Well, why don't you just keep that old screwdriver, then? We don't need it."

"No, ma'am; he wouldn't let me."

"Well, for goodness sakes. All right, now you be careful, you hear?"

Lee took off running. He had a chance to salvage the trip, earning credit with the director and at least some of the girls. He saw then that Cecil had himself fetched a wrench and screwdriver from somewhere, and already was at work with a flashlight that presumably he had bor-rowed as well. Meantime on board the bus, the other mu-sicians had taken out their sandwiches and Orange Drinks and were enjoying themselves in the conditions there.

Gorge rising, he went to the director and, taking his courage, spoke out loud and clear: "I did what you said."

"Hm?"

"Borrowed a screwdriver!"

"Good, good. You didn't borrow a reed, too, did you?"

That did it. Lee stomped off and went a few feet down the highway before turning and coming back. In his clarinet case he had packed a cheeseburger and pickle, assuming no one had confiscated them already. And yet, all-in-all, he still preferred to be out here with Cecil and the adult than in there with seventh and eighth-grade people.

Followed then another ten minutes during which no one had anything to say, which is to say until 1:15, when Cecil came out and began brushing off the leaves and mud. He had injured himself and had a significant amount of blood betwixt his knuckles. Lee had seen this before when dealing with nuts and bolts.

"Think it'll be all right now," he said modestly, wearing a rugged expression.

"Told you," Lee said. "Told you he could fix it."

"Yes, you did."

"Shoot, he could fix an *airplane*, if he had to!"

"Okay, calm down, Lee. Now let's see if we can get this thing rolling again."

They all climbed on board, Lee, Cecil, and the adult. It was not in the driver's contract to do mechanical work, and in fact the man was too busy with his own lunch, which included a beverage of some kind in a Mason jar.

"Gracious," said the girl, who now once again was sitting just behind him, "you're drenched!"

"Naw, I'm used to it."

"And I think Cecil is bleeding!" she went on, whispering the information.

"Yeah, but we don't care about stuff like that."

Outside the rain continued, assailing the roof. Let him have a set of dry clothes and cup of hot chocolate and he might have been perfectly happy just now. That was when the bandleader rose and worked his way down the aisle, bringing to Lee his golden uniform.

"Get those clothes off," he ordered "and get into your costume. 'Less you want to get pneumonia. Where's Cecil?"

Lee pointed to him, a wounded figure seated in the extreme corner of the bus. To him the bandleader now turned, startled to find him seated next to a girl he had never seen before.

"Oh, good."

"It's okay; I invited her."

"Good, good. Let me see that wound."

Cecil removed the girl's handkerchief and displayed the injury, a not very serious affair that had worked its way along the base of his thumb.

"You'll need a couple of stitches."

"Naw, shoot no."

"Okay, here's your uniform. Go ahead and put it on now before you get . . ."

"Pneumonia," Lee helped.

They were left alone, Cecil and Lee, along with the three boys and two girls who shared that region. In the matter of changing clothes, Lee would have preferred to be left alone; instead, Cecil immediately hefted off his shirt and already was unlinking his belt when the girls got up and ran away.

The uniform, a bright yellow business made from a corded material of some kind, was heavy and warm and had braid on it, the most splendid suit he'd ever possess. Looking straight forward in his soldierly fashion, he counted slowly to ten and then turned and spoke to Cecil: "Hey, Cecil."

"Hm?" He was smoking without using his hands—it was only the third or fourth time that Lee had seen him do that—while the other hand, the one left over, was wrapped around Gwen.

"I forgot to take the screwdriver back."

"No hope for a dope."

Relieved, Lee sheltered his eyes and scanned the area behind him, an obscure realm still occupied by the ninth-grade girl he presumed.

"I wadn't sure we'd be able to fix it," said Lee, squinting into the dim.

"But you did, though."

"I'm not saying it was easy."

"Well, I guess not!"

"But everything seems to be all right now."

She laughed out loud at him. She had finished her Orange Drink, and the empty bottle was wont to roll about on the floor until she retrieved it and put it elsewhere. Next to her, Cecil had gotten into a kiss with Gwen and was drawing it out to maximum length. Lee counted up to six and kept on going, stopping only when he came to thirteen, the longest kiss he had ever seen.

"They're in love," he said, whispering to the dark girl. "And so it's okay."

"I know."

They looked at each other.

They came into the city of Tuscaloosa at just after four and drove through the grounds of the world-famous university named after the state. Lee hewed to the window, impatient to catch a view of some of the college coed girls and varsity football players who characterized this particular town. He spied an old man walking a dog, and when that passed from view, two male youths, one of them in glasses. They passed a brick building in which some dozen scientific-looking persons were hovering over an experiment of some kind, to judge from the white coats they were wearing. The brains of these people, their dedication—he began to feel quite small again when he compared himself.

"Look at that one," Cecil whispered, indicating an elderly man in a beard. "You think you're so smart, shit, he
could spell every word there is. They got *microscopes* in
there, too. See 'em? And *women*. Shit, they got more
women here than you could . . ."

Gwen hit him. The radio meantime was giving off the
same sort of music familiar to him from his own
hometown. Radiating in all directions, the beautiful "Tennessee Waltz" had crossed the Coosa already on its long
journey across the South. It made Lee proud that his little
slice of life had been cut from the 1950s. On the other
hand, Tuscaloosa itself seemed wrongly configured, the
authorities having chosen to harbor their negroes *east* of
town.

Came now the downtown section, stores on top of
stores, beauty parlors and a government building. Lee was
interested in a Woolworth's that took up the better part of
a block, and next to that a hardware and fishing tackle
outlet. He did not expect at this particular time to find a
hobby shop selling stamps and coins, and in fact he never
did come across such a place during his whole stay in Tuscaloosa. He perceived a pool hall with some of the same
kind of people in it as in the halls of his own hometown—
lean men fond of whiskey who rarely shaved. Saw a fat
woman carrying too many bundles, and behind her a lost
boy who only just now seemed to recognize that he was
following the wrong mother. And then, finally, saw a boy
of a certain type and kind who was so much like himself
that it gave Lee an uncanny feeling. Apparently, they had
been growing up analogously, side-by-side as it were, albeit on opposite sides of Alabama. They looked at each other.

The bus stopped at an intersection in the core of the
city and idled quietly as the bandleader got to his feet and
spoke: "All right, yes, we're here. And you've got just exactly
. . ."—he glanced at his watch—". . . exactly two hours and

twelve minutes before you're on stage. Yes? And so we'll meet *right here*"—he bent and touched the floor with his index finger—"right here at five o'clock exactly. What did I say, Charlie?"

"Five o'clock."

"Good! Five o'clock and not one minute later. You read me, Cecil?"

"Yes, sir."

"Five o'clock, American time."

They agreed to it. Leland's heart had meantime begun to palpitate. He checked for his wallet and pencil box, finding that he had left one of them behind. Never had he been so far from native ground. Coming to the head of the line, he stepped down into the living Tuscaloosa, and after testing the sidewalk, brought his other foot with him.

He noticed several things at once, but especially the people. He saw an old man pushing a carriage full of groceries in lieu of children. Where was Cecil? An unleashed dog now came up and, after analyzing Leland's shoes, turned and went the other way. He began to feel confused, Lee did, caught up in this gyre of activity. Saw a blind negro with an accordion, dark glasses, and a begging cup. Putting on a bored expression, Lee marched straight forward for a distance of about fifty yards, ignoring the world around him until he ran up against a pawnshop window full of a variety of things. He saw knives with ten-inch blades, a box of watches and chains, a dozen leather-bound books, rings and pins, and—and here he stopped—a stamp album opened to Lithuania.

It hurt him to see a thing like that. A thousand years might go by before he'd have the cash to buy a collection like that—complicated, well-organized, and loaded with rarities. Or perhaps he could overcome his liking for such things and learn to hate them instead, a test of his increasing Will. Suddenly he jumped back, surprised to find the expelled boy Clarence standing at his side. He wasn't supposed to have come along.

"I seen you standing over here."

"Yeah," Lee said.

"Look at all that shit. Hey, I wouldn't mind having that one," he said, indicating toward one of the knives with a forest scene engraved on the blade. "Shit!"

Lee agreed. He had rather hoped the boy might move away now and go about his business; instead, he came up nearer to Lee and examined his face.

"What's the deal with you, actually? And where's that goddamn little box you're always carrying around?"

"I left it," Lee said, pointing toward the bus."

"Well, well. Is that a fact? So you decided to carry that screwdriver instead."

"Yeah."

"You stole anything yet?"

"I just got here!"

"Yeah, me too."

Lee looked off. He could not understand why this person wanted to link up with him, who had not stolen anything in years. The boy came nearer.

"Say, what are you *worrying about* all the time—that's what I want to know. Hey, you want to go over yonder"—he pointed to the Woolworth's mentioned earlier—"and steal some stuff?"

Lee didn't want to. "Sure," he said.

Later on, looking back upon it, he would have said the place had more merchandise in it than he had thought. And then, too, this time he had come with a full dollar bill, the gift of his father. It provided him a choice of buying or stealing, depending upon conditions.

"Hey! Don't be following me around all the time, okay?"

They separated, the other boy moving off quickly toward the rear of the store. Himself, Lee was in the market for a billfold, a leather one with pockets in it, a long-time desideratum of his. Encouraged by the dearth of sales-women, he strolled past a counter of yo-yos, comic books, and other unguarded artifacts that would have appealed to him as recently as several months ago, before he had gone bad. Came next a pile of female purses, and then at the very bottom of the counter, an appreciable selection of men's paraphernalia, including wallets, cufflinks, tie clasps, and the like. Changing over into a naïve expres-sion, he picked up one item after another and looked them over in such a way as to suggest that he didn't know what they were. The woman, a tired-looking quantity in a dress, smiled at him perfunctorily and then went back to gazing out over his head to the outside traffic. It ought to be easy, Lee thought, to take one of the billfolds by ex-changing it for his own. Half a minute went by as he stood waiting for his nerves to settle. Across the way a woman and child were smiling at his uniform, while fifty yards further on Clarence had taken up an air rifle and was aim-ing it at various people in the store.

He gathered up a wallet, Lee, and explored it for pock-ets and hidden places. No one was watching, or anyway no one with authority enough to arrest him. His inclination was to return the thing to its place and abandon the store to Clarence; instead, without thinking very clearly about it, he threw the thing into his back pocket, arranging it face-to-face with his existing wallet.

He thought that he would faint. He felt a headache coming on. But both of these problems soon faded away, and in their place he experienced a strange and very evil exultation that he had felt before upon certain occasions. Head held high, his face giving off a somewhat indignant expression, he exited the place and strolled very slowly down the sidewalk for about fifty yards in one direction and twenty in another.

"What'd you git?" Clarence asked, once they had found

each other. He was three years older than Lee, his teeth were bad, and he wore a continual expression that made it seem he was suffering from gas.

"Billfold."

"Show me."

Lee showed it.

"Okay, that's all right. You're one of us now."

Himself, the boy had stolen some half-dozen candy bars, one of which he now handed off to Lee.

"Want to go back? Steal some more?"

Lee didn't want to. "Sure."

They entered from long distance, each boy choosing the portal that best comported with him. There was a girl in there—Lee hadn't noticed her earlier—a girl. Of course, he could not be sure that she would admire his uniform or whether, like some people, she would point and grin. That was when he discovered Charlie T. on the far side of the store, where he was very obviously confiscating some items of his own. World enough and time, they could have cleaned out the whole store—this was the realization that now came over Lee. Never had Tuscaloosa seen such people.

They gathered on the sidewalk, joined this time by Charlie T.

"What'd you git?"

"Two more wallets."

"Gimme one."

Lee handed it over. Charlie had taken a plastic box full of drill bits, but had not managed to come away with the drill itself. Meantime the day had turned perceptibly cooler, and to defray the chill they all three were eating candy bars while standing about and looking at each another.

"Want to go back?"

"No!" Lee started to say. "Sure."

But this time the girl was gone. Accordingly, he trod up and down the aisle for a certain time, aware that the woman no longer was casting maternal smiles in his direction. She was smart. He yawned, checked his watch, and then took up a paperback book, opened it, and sampled the writing, hoping in this way to divert the lady from Charlie T. working the next aisle. Outside, he saw other band members from other schools, some in uniform, others not, others chewing gum and some not. They included a girl in a kepi, a baton, and a skirt that was shorter even than those in his own hometown. Having completed the first paragraphs, Lee shut the book with a disappointed expression and returned to the out-of-doors, where Clarence was waiting for him.

"What'd you git?"

"Nothing."

"Chickenshit."

"I was helping Charlie T.! Anyway, what did *you* get?"

The boy looked off in the two directions, and after turning his back to the street, slowly and mysteriously rolled up his sleeve. Lee jumped back—three separate wristwatches running up his arm.

"Good Lord!"

"Would you just kindly shut up, for Christ's sakes! You get me in trouble, and I'll have to beat the shit out of you."

Charlie came up. He had still not succeeded in taking the drill set which, in any case, weighed several pounds.

"Want to go back in?"

"No," said Lee, using his real voice. "Besides, it's getting late."

"It ain't *that* late."

"It's *pretty* late."

That was true.

"And besides, I'm getting hungry."

"You just had a candy bar, for Christ's sakes!"

But Lee's attention was for a group of negro band people, some twenty of them or more, moving down the sidewalk. Their uniforms were purple with crimson streaks, and each member wore a plumed hat with a glossy bill—the best outfit Lee had ever seen.

"Good Lord!" he whispered. "Look at 'em!"

"Shit!"

"Hey, how come they get to wear those? Shit, that's a *lot* better than what we got."

"No, that's just the way things are these days. Don't get me started."

They stood aside, allowing the black musicians to pass by in their lofty fashion, an uppity people in feathers and gold.

"Look at 'em. Say, how come they always get everything while us, we don't get *nothing!*"

"Yeah, and we're the ones what have to pay for it. Taxes."

"Well, leastwise you ain't paying no taxes on them wallets."

That was true. A restaurant had come up on the left-hand side, a big one with a plate glass window facing the road. It startled him to see people eating in full view, a form of advertisement, he had to suppose, designed to show off the food. Coming nearer, he locked eyes with a fat man in a bib, his fork heavy-laden and suspended in mid-air. It was steak he was eating, steak pure and simple, along with a pale green beverage with a detritus of some kind floating on top.

"Look at that steak," Charlie said, coming nearer and pointing to it. "Bleeding, it looks like to me."

"He likes it that way."

"Shit, I bet that old bastard eats steak every day."

"Yeah. And his *eyes* are fat, too."

(They were.)

"Good Lord. Feel sorry for his wife."

"Yeah. 'Course now we don't know what *she* looks like."

"Wife, my ass. What, would *you* marry him?"

They came nearer. The man was showing signs of irritation. Smitty had glued his face to the glass and was making evil faces at a distance of about eighteen inches from the actual person.

There were other people in the window, most of them more or less normal-looking for Tuscaloosa. He saw a boy and his family—two standard adults and an eleven- or twelve-year-old with an angelic face. He was weak, Lee was certain of it, and didn't have anything remotely like the sort of spiritual force that Lee demanded in people. Yea, and someday he (Lee) would be able to enter crowded buildings and know that he was the best man there.

The area was noisier than they had expected, and they had to wait an appreciable time before at last the hostess came, looked them over disappointedly, and then conducted them to a booth far enough from the window that no Tuscaloosians would have to see them. The menu was a massive affair as big as a newspaper, and had a picture of a swan on it. Lee had one bill in his original wallet, a bequest from his father. The menu had nothing as cheap as that.

"Shit!" (Smitty) "Look at them prices!"

"No, that's just the way it is these days. Nothing surprises me anymore."

"And what the hell is this?" Clarence asked, trying and failing to read the French. Lee noticed that they were being watched.

"Maybe we ought to leave."

"I ain't leaving!"

"Me neither," Lee said. "Heck, no."

Five minutes went by as they went through the pages of the beige-colored brochure with its ribbon and coat of arms. Bored with it, and having given up on the French, Clarence had taken out a deck of playing cards (stolen) and was checking through them carefully, as if looking for missing numbers. Two tables away, Lee's glance settled upon a middle-aged lady sitting in such a way that a person could see deep into her mouth and part way up her nose, had anyone wanted. They had less than an hour to fodder themselves and return to the bus. Suddenly (and here Lee's heart leapt up in joy), Cecil came and claimed a chair, followed shortly by his girl.

"Okay, boys," he said. "Let's see what you got."

They were cautious about showing what they had stolen, which is to say until Lee shyly drew out one of his wallets and laid it in general view.

"What's this?"

"Billfold."

"Yeah, but they ain't no money in it? Nothing, right?"

True. Lee took it back and returned it to its place. He was waiting for Smitty to show his watches; instead, that was when Cecil seized upon Gwen's purse, opened it, and showed several large pieces of female jewelry. It was just like him—stealing on behalf of others.

"Good Lord!"

"Sure. We need it more than they do."

Outside a policeman walked past, a heavy person with a stick, a sullen face, and an unknown attitude toward musicians. Came then the waitress, a shriveled person with, however, a great pile of iridescent hair that sparkled in the obscurity. No one had been born to look like that. And then, too, her face wore an annoyed expression. Cecil looked at her, called her "honey," and then, after drawing leisurely on his cigar, ordered two cheeseburgers and as many Orange Drinks. The woman made a face and let her writing pad hang at her side.

"You fellows ought to try Herbie's. They have what you want."

"And two pieces of chocolate pie." (He was also ordering for Gwen—it was like him.)

Slowly, the waitress brought her writing pad up to where she could write on it.

"And you?"

"I don't want nothing," Clarence said.

"He'll take a cheeseburger," Cecil said.

"And Orange Drink."

"Me, too." (Smitty.)

The woman now shifted her gaze to Lee. Smaller than the others, his chin came up to the tabletop and no further. He did love the privacy of booths, especially when they were populated by the three or four persons he would naturally have chosen for that purpose.

"Cheeseburger," Lee ordered.

"And Orange Drink?"

He thought about it, opting for the affirmative after a few moments had gone by. Across the way, the fat man was deep into an ice cream preparation of some sort and had gotten some of the material on his nose. For Lee, this was the time to transfer his personal papers over into his new wallet, a nerve-wracking process that required him to make a series of decisions as to where each thing most aptly fitted. He was fastidious, a trait that seemed to annoy his tablemates.

"Look at him. Piddling around over there."

"He's nervous."

"Hell, yeah, he's nervous! He lives inside a glass ball, is what he told me."

"You got to get over that, Sloan. If you want to be one of us."

"It's his liver."

"There ain't nothing wrong with that liver. Anyway, I'd rather be like him than like you," the girl said, turning and looking directly into Cecil's face. "*He's* got a future."

"I don't got a future?"

"Nope. None of us do."

They laughed. Lee laughed, too, who was beginning to feel better in light of what the girl had said. Later on, assuming he was still living, he would make it a point to help them with their futures.

The food, when it came, turned out to be exactly what was needed. Cecil could eat no onions, and his girl could eat no cheese; between the two of them, they flushed both burgers down with Orange Drinks. As for Clarence, he had not eaten in days, and with Cecil paying, he managed to consume two of the things in a shorter time than Lee could form a bib out of the enormous napkin with the image of a swan on it. Smitty meantime had pushed back and was smoking on a cigarette, a long, brown, and very thin item of his own manufacture that sizzled and popped whenever the flame came into touch with the inferior tobacco. Soon, within half an hour or less, they would be on stage and in front of hundreds of people, a development that made Lee shiver.

"Cecil?"

"Hm?" (They had finished their burgers, Gwen and he, and had both drawn off into the corner, where they were smooching with each other in plain open view.)

"We don't have much time."

The boy didn't answer. He had his right hand on the girl's waist, or in other words about midway between her two female regions. His eyes were open, but the girl's were closed, the reversal of the way Lee would want it.

"We're supposed to be on the bus in . . . nineteen minutes."

"Lee?"

"Yes?"

"Shut up."

Lee went back to his wallet. He had a photo of his former dog, the best of a long line, now dead. Had the signed certificate of a Boy Scout merit badge in archery, a legal permit allowing him to drive an outboard motor, and a dollar bill. Had a silver medal with the engraving of an eagle on it and two faded coins that had set up impressions of themselves in the leather of his original wallet. Had other things as well, including a newspaper article that described a long-ago action of one of his uncles in another part of the state. All these he put away in the best-fitting compartments and then handed off the obsolete wallet to Clarence, who took it without a word. Gwen, he saw, was wearing the necklace given her by Cecil, a complex artifact in which the various beads and seashells had been dipped in several kinds of paint. "We've only got fourteen minutes!" Lee started to say, before changing his mind and saying nothing. The fat man had gone, leaving behind a full dollar tip scrolled up in the handle of his coffee cup, the largest gratuity that ever Lee had seen.

They hit the road as darkness came and began to move at speed against the grain of the pedestrians, a bored-looking people who appeared to be moving away from, instead of toward, the concert hall. Arriving at the bus, Lee went direct to his place, where the girl was missing. He had seven minutes and not one moment more to lubricate the joints of his clarinet and put the thing together. Already Cecil had taken out his trumpet, had burnished it, and was blowing a few notes from the top of the register, a fierce noise that sounded like screaming. Suddenly the bus lurched and ran forward a few yards before turning into a side street that might almost be too narrow to negotiate. Among the noise of this mobile rehearsal, Lee could pick out Steven's saxophone, certain members of the trombone section, and Smitty's snare drum giving off a funereal sound. The driver was drunk, or at any rate intoxicated, judging by his face in the mirror. That was when someone tapped Lee on the shoulder, causing him to realize that the girl had been there all along, lurking in the dark. They grinned at each other. His impulse was to jump on top of her while the band was playing; instead he pulled out his new wallet and showed it to her.

"Oh!" she said. "You didn't steal that, did you?"

"Sure."

"You're so bad. What are we going to do with you?"

She was not as indignant as she might have been. Suddenly, recognizing that he was talking face to face with a ninth grader, he began to tremble.

"I didn't steal as much as Cecil!"

"Well, I reckon not! Anyway, I won't tell."

There was no further question now, but that she, too, had some evil in her, and it was sparkling in her eyes. Further, she had put on her saffron braided uniform, giving her a look that was both military and yet girlish at one and the same time.

"I don't have a reed," he said.

"Poor thing. What are you going to do?"

"I don't know. Get into trouble, I guess."

"You're *always* getting into trouble, aren't you?"

It was true. Close to tears, Lee nodded and gazed off into a crowd of moribund adults sitting about in a coffee shop. The bus meanwhile was running down an alley inside the city of Tuscaloosa, making loud music wherever they went.

The hall, when they came to it, looked a great deal to him like a photograph of General Washington's home in Mount Vernon. With his hair standing up on ends and his nerves about ready to finish him off, he exited the bus with a bored expression and fell into Cecil's shadow. It bothered him that another band, bigger than his own, was just now leaving the place in a spirit of glee, as if they had won the blue ribbon already and were carrying it home. They passed in silence, which is to say until the two opposing squads of woodwinds encountered each other on the sidewalk. He heard a snide comment coming from the bassoonist, a large boy with red hair and a face like a northern Yankee's. Lee waited.

"Y'all might just as well go on home," this boy announced, planting himself in the middle of the walk. "Shit, we've already won all the prizes."

"Ha, ha, ha," Preston said. "You don't have any idea!"

"What'd you say?"

"Idea."

"Oh, leave him alone," said one of the girls. (Always trying to make peace, girls were, it seemed to Lee.) "Anyway, it don't matter."

"Don't matter? Don't matter? You heard what he said!"

By now the two bands were bogged down halfway between the building and the highway. Preston wanted an end to it.

"I guess we'll just have to see about that," he said.

"You bet we'll see! Shit, you people couldn't play your way out of a wet paper bag!"

"What'd you say?"

"Bag."

"Okay, that does it. Just wait right here, okay? Will you?"

"Sure! What'cha going to do, go get somebody else?"

Cecil was near to the head of the line. Leaving him in reserve, Lee continued on to Reese and tugged at his belt, getting his attention.

"He insulted us," Lee said, stuttering. "Said we couldn't play our way out of a wet paper bag!"

"Who?"

"Guy over there. See him?"

"*That* one?"

"Yeah, that's it! Said we don't know how to play!"

He groaned wearily, Reese, but then disaggregated his arm from the majorette's and began to follow Lee. Lee had always appreciated the way he would march up to people, first spitting on the ground and then going up to within half a foot of the person.

"You got something you want to say?"

The Yankee took on a pinched expression. "I was talking to him."

"Talk to me."

Several things now began to happen: first, the girls had

continued toward the building and would not look back; two, Reese's left hand was opening and shutting, sometimes forming a fist and sometimes looking like a spatula; three, Lee was saying, "Hit him! You can do it!"; and four, the bandleader was working his way toward them.

The auditorium itself was capacious and had many green-covered seats in it. Lee counted somewhere between five hundred and a thousand people in it, most of them musicians from other schools. One last time he searched for a reed, looking beneath the upholstery in the little padded suitcase that held his horn. He needed to urinate, a concomitant of having very soon to go up on stage without a reed. His last consolation—that the band currently on stage was worse than his own. Bending nearer, he could detect certain musical derelictions in the performance, as also in the rather tawdry uniforms that tended to blur any distinction between the boys and girls. As to the conductor—(Lee wanted to laugh)—he was a frightened-looking little man in glasses, the sort his own teacher could have destroyed with a single blow.

"Not very good, are they?" said Lee to the boy next to him, a pale individual supposed to be an oboist, also in glasses.

The boy never answered, wherefore Lee turned to his left, finding there that same Mildred Weston who abominated the sight of him.

"Not very good, are they?" he submitted.

Mildred never answered, not until several seconds had gone by.

"Are you going to talk? Or listen?"

"Talk."

"Then go sit somewhere else."

Lee never moved. In the meantime Steve was blowing silently into his fist, preparing for his solo as Lee supposed. Himself, he had more lief to forfeit one arm and one leg respectively than stand up in front of a mass of ungrateful people while striving to make music on a non-functioning clarinet. Just then, through the open doors, a new orchestra began to file inside, this one with a harpist in a snow-white toga. He loved her. Sadly, she was being followed and proceeded by scads of crude-looking boys, trombonists and the like, with scuff marks on them. A lily among wiregrass, she seemed to him, reminding him of the sad fate that lay in wait for women and girls.

Followed then a certain interval, more or less, during which a violin quartet went up on stage and played the sort of music appropriate to that instrument. Lee, focusing on the harpist, perceived how her hair had been done up in a mass of curls that rested lightly on her collar, her neck, and still other curls. As to her underlying personality, he could determine only so much from her profile, but what he did determine looked satisfactory to him, certainly. That was when the quartet suddenly stood up and waited for the applause, which was thin and seemed to come from far away. Soon, within thirty seconds or less, his own organization would rise and walk toward the stage.

Having arisen, Lee hurried forward and fell in behind Cecil. His habit, Cecil's, was to carry his trumpet like a football where no one could get at it. Lee spoke up loud and clear, getting the boy's attention: "Well, I guess this is it."

"Yup."

"I doubt we'll win anything."

"Wait a minute, you aren't getting *nervous* on me again, are you?"

Lee snorted and waved it away.

"I don't know about you, Sloan."

"But what if we don't win anything?"

"Well, I guess we'll just have to go outside and dig a hole for ourseffs."

Cheered, Lee changed positions, carrying his horn as it were a bottle of Orange Drink. The stage was further than he had expected, higher, taller, and took up a greater deal of space. The audience had turned into a plethora of little round heads with eyes and other features. The band members now seated themselves, bringing it off with considerable aplomb. He saw some of the worst boys wearing some of the most serious expressions. If he himself should do badly, or rather make no sound at all, perhaps the audience would think the silence had come from elsewhere. Putting on an annoyed expression, he placed the screwdriver beneath the chair and pretended to take out the fresh new reed he lacked and lock it into place. The concert was to endure for twenty minutes, a considerable time in some respects. He turned to Smitty, who seemed on the verge of falling off to sleep.

"What time is it?" Lee whispered.

The boy awoke, checked his watches, and then used up several moments to calculate the average time. It was his style to play much too loudly on his drums, a trait that might help to disguise Lee's inevitable silence. It was then that Chichi dropped his mouthpiece on the floor and had to crawl for it; except for that, the hall was silent. Lee waited for the conductor to lift his arms, hold them there for a long time, and then set the music going. Lee, his cheeks bulging from the pressure, blew strenuously into his horn, actually creating a small noise somewhat like a cricket's. He had not played twenty notes before he realized that he was going to be all right, that no one noticed, that the trumpets were carrying the burden, and what a relief it was to be among allies and friends.

They won no ribbons on that day. Lee, hopping and skipping down the sidewalk, ran to get on board the bus before anyone could preempt his position in the rear. It was well past seven o'clock at night, and the city was speckled with bright, gaudy neon lights. Suddenly Lee spun about and tried to initiate a discussion with the girl behind him, till forced to see that she hadn't gotten on board as yet. The last he wanted was for some seventh-grader or trombone player, or something like that, to take her place.

"Well," he said, turning toward Cecil, "I guess we didn't win any ribbons."

"Next year."

Next year they would both be eighth-graders. A thousand years might go by, and they'd always be traveling to Tuscaloosa each and every year—such was Lee's unexamined expectation at that particular time.

"Think I'll start playing the trumpet," he said thoughtfully, looking out into the night.

"What you need is a *reed*."

The bus was mostly full by now, but still he hadn't caught sight of the girl, not until she spoke up from the dark domain in the extreme corner where she had been abiding all the time.

"I reckon he can play a trumpet if he wants to," she said.

He recognized the voice and, coming closer, recognized the lower left quadrant of her face that had partially emerged from the shadows. If he could just once get a clear full view of her whole person at the same time, his desire then to jump on top of her probably would be even greater than it was now. Up front, the radio was tuned to a local program of high quality where "Why Don't You Believe Me?" was playing. Using his Will, he asked to hear it again, but was given "Wheel of Fortune" instead. Previously Preston had been sitting with Mattie Lou, and it interested Lee to see that he had changed over to Lois, where they were whispering about something or another. Their profiles, viewed against the night, were those of a gander and a goose, or like cardboard cutouts or, more accurately—they were still wearing their official hats—like a tea kettle and a coffee pot. As for the conductor, his profile was smaller than it used to be, the result of the band's performance, as Lee believed. Suddenly the bus lurched out into the traffic and drove away.

"Hey! Where's Clarence?" someone asked.

Lee could see where at least three people were smoking cigarettes, even if he could not readily name them in the dark. He heard a noise that sounded like a girl slapping someone's face. Worst of all was the driver, thoroughly drunk by now. He teetered from side to side. Outside, a tall man standing in the intersection tried briefly but unavailingly to force open one of the windows on that side. But they were too fast for him. They had come into an area of highly granulated neon, a fluid substance that ran into the alleys and was reflected in pools of ink. Even now some of the Tuscaloosians were still at work, still laboring in the upper stories of office buildings. He saw a worried-looking man hunched over a desk, and then a woman in an apron using a broom. This was the adult world, a form of life in which a ride by twilight aboard a bus was no doubt a routine matter. Saw a coed pacing homeward hurriedly—(where is she now?)—with two books cradled in her arms. And a policeman wearing sunglasses in the pitch-black night. He shivered, Lee, saying, "Good Lord, I've still got another sixty or seventy years for things like this!"

His arrogance increased. He was sitting on the next-to-last seat of a Ford-built bus somewhere in Alabama in late October of that year. He had needed eleven years to arrive at this point, and things could get only better as time went on. He turned to look at Gwen, who smiled right back, giving him the sort of maternal glance he loved to see in ninth-grade women. Cecil himself was half asleep, but ready at all times to come awake in case of emergency. And the next he knew, they had broken out of the city and into the ambient countryside.

The bus was so fast, so strongly put together, so pressurized and waterproof that he began to imagine they were on board a submarine gliding at high speed above the ocean floor. Strange creatures, squids and octopuses, pressed at the windows and tried to look inside. He saw a ruined fortress and broken tower, as at first he had let himself believe, and then the yellow Moon itself, a frail structure crumbling into dust. Telephone poles came running and jumping past, and then a few scuttled farms that had settled to the bottom of the sea. Later on, laughing back upon it, he would remember it as only the third "pre-experience" (pre-aesthetic experience) to have been vouchsafed him.

Up front, the beautiful "Tennessee Waltz" had played twice in succession, followed then by "Ebb Tide," "Harbor Lights," and "Red Sails in the Sunset." It made Lee bitter, knowing in advance that this journey must someday end. There were twenty souls on board that bus, each with a profile unique to him or her alone. They rode then though a small town in which everyone either had gone to sleep or else was sitting in darkness on their porches. Just then, a raccoon or opossum stepped out into the road and fired back at them with amber rays extruding from its eyes. The woods were dark and deep and full of beings enduring lives of constant insecurity. That was when Cecil bent forward and whispered in his ear, "You okay?"

"Yeah."

"You need to calm down some."

"I will," he said.

He didn't. There was a ninth-grader sitting not more than twenty-seven inches behind him, a pretty one lucubrating in the shadows. He let a few seconds go by and then turned and, sheltering his eyes, began scanning for her in the dark.

"I'm here," she said.

"I guess we didn't win any ribbons."

She laughed.

"The driver's drunk. That's why we're going so fast."

"I like it that way."

"Me, too."

They grinned evilly at one another. He could see her right eye, or part of it anyway, and the gleaming bill of her military hat. The next minutes went past slowly, both of them still looking at one another. Gwen had fallen asleep on Cecil's shoulder, allowing him to guard over her while he was smoking. There was yet another person of some sort on the back bench whom Lee hadn't seen before. He caught a glimpse, Lee, of a minor meteorite falling to earth slightly north of Vance. He was also aware that the ninth-grade girl had moved somewhat closer to him, so much so in fact that their two heads were but about ten inches apart.

"I saw a falling star," he said.

"Oh, you did not."

"I'm not saying it was a real big one."

"Oh! You'd say anything, wouldn't you?"

He admitted that he would. Just now they were about nine inches apart. Meantime Cecil had turned his attention to them and was watching closely.

"She wants you to kiss her, Slade," said Cecil, using his new favorite name for the boy who did his homework.

Lee waved it away. They were not *that* close, not yet.

"It's up to him," the girl said.

Lee trembled. They were seven inches apart, possibly less, and he could clearly make out her lips, indisputably those of a girl. They were just simply different from each other, boys and girls, and meantime she was a person in her own right with inclinations of her own. He now recognized that fourth person, a former friend of his.

"You going to kiss her? Or not?"

"Haven't decided."

"You better. You don't get a chance like this every day, for Pete's sakes!"

It was true that she seemed to be waiting. He could see no actual harm in coming as close to her as she already had come to him, a gambit that put them about three inches apart. No other falling stars were to be seen at this particular time.

"Do it!"

Lee came nearer, giving her the concentrated attention that women, according to his sources, actually crave. By this time, their lips were actually touching, and he was able to testify to the pressure that hers applied to his. Six seconds went by in this condition while the half-dozen persons who had gathered about cheered him on. She did *not* move away, neither did she retreat in any direction, the most brazen behavior he had seen since being assaulted by that high school girl in the Canteen. Having now finished with one kiss, he came back for more.

"Alright!" Cecil said. "Don't stop now."

"I won't."

He was beginning to understand the attraction of it. It was not the very first time for him, and yet he was far from being bored. By now the girl had actually placed one of her hands on the back of his head and was using it egregiously to increase the pressure. And just how many other things had she not already done in her fourteen years? Loins benumbed, he grew dizzy with excitement.

"Keep it up, Sloan. She likes it."

"Me, too."

Laughter from several places. Suddenly the girl drew back to take a breath, wasted time as it seemed to him. Reaching out, he was able to take her by the neck and bring her back.

"Look at Lee!"

"Yeah. He's one of us now."

Again the girl drew back. Lee could feel his gorge rising.

"Hey!"

"No, you've had enough."

"I have not!"

Laughter.

"Wait till next year. When you're older."

Next year? He wanted to cry. Also it seemed to him that some of the others were beginning to lose interest in what he was doing, a tendency he had noticed before in people.

"Okay, one more, okay?" he said loudly, trying to bring them back.

The girl laughed, came forward, and gave him a brief one that endured for hardly more than a second or two. Next thing he knew, she had drawn back into her shadows, where he was never to see her again.

The evening now came on in full force, bringing with it clouds darker than the night. Darker still were Alabama's two varieties of bats, great ones and small, searching desperately across the sky. Itself, the Moon had separated into three unequal pieces, where they appeared on the brink of going out entirely. Turned he then toward the north-northeast, where he caught tonight's first view of the gleaming lava streams running down old *Epsilon*, largest of the volcanoes that lay over against Jacksonville. At the same time, he half-hoped to see the stars form themselves into the likenesses of historic faces, Confederate generals and people like that. And yet his aesthetic development was not quite as advanced as that, not at that particular time, at any rate. Next, he turned to speak to Cecil, but then decided not to say anything when he recognized that the boy and girl had lapsed off to sleep in one another's arms.

It might be that everyone was asleep, everyone but him. Nor did he expect to sleep, not after today, and not for a long, long time to come. Accordingly, he came out of

his berth and went forward, checking each and every face
one by one insofar as the Moon allowed it.

Seven

Retiring early (and rising early, too), he got through
the next four and a half weeks without further slippage.
His stamp collection, built on borrowed money, was also
thriving, especially in the Sino-Japanese region. (Later on,
looking back upon it, he was to remember his surprise
when he found that these were two distinct societies, each
with a writing system of its own. [Earlier still he had
thought the Sun and Moon were one and the same disc,
albeit in two modalities. {And dogs and cats the male and
female of a single species.}])

He needed three days to organize the above-referenced
stamps and then one day more to leave school early on a
dental excuse, and hurry off downtown to see *The Adventures of Robin Hood* for the third time. He admitted it,
that he had perhaps allowed himself to become overly focused on this historical personage who had so amazingly
and with such attention to detail prefigured his own personality and career. Both these people had been destined
for heroism, even if perforce Lee would have to carry out
his part without benefit of background music. And then,
too, the weather was getting chill, and he had to hurry
home from the theater, arriving sixteen minutes too late
for *Sky King*.

He loved to run past the Christmas decorations, the
ornamented trees, the strings of lights, and at least two
places showing cardboard Santas disappearing into chimneys with bags of gifts. This was not the largest of Alabama's cities, and yet the spirit here was superior even to
Tuscaloosa. Halfway home, he stopped to gaze upon a tree
that had been painted white and adorned with blue lights
only, the loneliest, remotest, and most dignified of all the

things he saw that night.

It pleased him to run into his own home (warm, stocked with food, dog), and then to assimilate the last minutes of his favorite radio program before Gabriel Heatter came on. Hunched in front of an instrument as big almost as a refrigerator, he loved to dial across the miles, sometimes happening upon Philadelphia or New York, where people spoke the way they did. His father meantime, mostly asleep by now, sat shriveled up in the corner of his chair, his cigarette ash ready to topple off onto the floor. The man had been laboring all day, but could look forward to a few hours of rest before having to arise and go off and toil away another day. It was the common fate.

Lee next turned his attention to his younger brother, a short personality with a large head and pale face who stood some ten feet away, watching everything. Finally, their mother, who took up the second-best chair—she was knitting or darning (he didn't know the difference) while wearing the little smile so characteristic of her when the family was together, warm, fed, and safe. As to the world outside with its cars and criminals, the noise of other people's radios and footsteps passing by—they knew nothing about the family and its private dealings. Which is to say until about nine when, suddenly, Steven burst through the front door and, after giving his regards to Leland's parents, asked to borrow a no. 2 lead pencil. That door was never locked, a Southern tradition that his father was unwilling to ignore. Besides, he had a .32 caliber revolver in his top drawer, where Lee was wont to take it out from time to time and show it to other boys.

He retired soon after, abandoning the radio to his parents. He had hoped to go to sleep instantaneously; instead he had to fight for it. He dreamt at first that he was walking across an open field, and when that threatened to bore him back to wakefulness, imagined himself aboard a submarine with a small crew of the people who were dearest to him. Ten minutes went by, the boat continually diving until it reached the very lowest level of the sea. Here, in utter silence, rocked gently by the currents, a person could sleep.

He woke with the day, got into his clothes, and then hurriedly undressed again when he saw that he had been mistaken about the actual time. He judged it at somewhere between midnight and dawn, the best of hours, when the malfeasance of the world was at its lowest ebb. His brother had also climbed into bed at some point during the foregoing evening, and when Lee propped himself on his elbow and inspected him more closely, he verified that the boy's eyelids had become translucent, an amazing development that allowed him to maintain vigil even at this hour. It chagrined Lee even more that a late-season moth had found a way into the room and was beating on the ceiling with two pairs of tattered wings. Outside a car drove past, casting contorted shadows that leapt from wall to wall. Sleep? In a world of stamps, heroes, girls, radio programs? He laughed out loud at the thought of it.

He waited until it really was day and then again transferred over into his clothes. A great shame, that people had bodies. Nor could he add up the time he had spent washing and brushing and the rest of all that. His brother had gone. Came then to him the scent of bacon, along with the somewhat more modulated smell of toast and eggs. His father had not had the rest he needed, and the woman remained silent as she hovered over the table in her robe. Unwilling to ask for any more money than he had already spent on stamps, Lee mentioned something about the need to replace his no. 2 lead pencil, a ploy that brought five cents.

He squandered several minutes waiting for Cherise to

come along, and when she wouldn't do so, proceeded on to school in a darkening mood. The day was cold, by his standards, and overcast, the sort of weather that up north would have been considered very good. No single persimmon still hewed to the topmost branches of Mrs. Jenson's tree; her Christmas decorations were superb, however. He then passed in front of a house that hadn't bothered even to set up a wreath on the door, nor tree in the parlor, nor anything. Gorge rising, he tried to understand the sort of people who declined to enter into the season. Because they wished to distance themselves from their neighbors? Or had given up on life entirely? Even his own father, as tired as he might be, had set up a high-quality tree.

He had come all the way to school without stepping on a single crack. But when he rounded the corner and saw that it was too cold to loiter in the yard, he went inside and stood with the seventh-graders huddled about the furnace. They actually looked better than normal, the girls in their scarves and coats and cold-burnished cheeks. He wished that every one of them belonged to him alone. He went to Lois and nudged her, who turned and gave him a smile, the first good event of that particular day.

"Cold!" he said.

"Well, no wonder."

"It's not *always* cold."

"But today it is. Silly."

He had no answer for that. She had put on a bit of lipstick, or perhaps the residue of a chap stick to protect her from the weather. Her eyelashes were dense, the way he liked them, and numbered in the dozens. He didn't expect much from her, however, and was excited when suddenly she bent closer and reported, "Naomi likes you."

"What?"

"Naomi! She told me."

Lee reeled. He had heard of this girl who at one time

had been affiliated with Cecil.

"She did not."

"She did! Okay, I'm not going to talk to you anymore."

"*Why* does she like me?"

The girl took him by the sleeve and drew him off a short distance.

"Because you're funny."

Lee grinned. There was some truth in that.

"You mean . . . ?

"Yes! And because Mr. Debardeleben is so mean to you."

"Oh." He drew her off a short distance further.

"She likes me a lot, or just a little bit?"

"I don't know. A lot, I guess."

Lee reeled. He had seen Naomi once or twice, here and there, and although he wouldn't have ranked her among the top two-thirds of girls, yet he did have a particular appreciation for people who would say what she had. There arose then in his mind the problem of what he was expected to do in light of this development.

"Does she like me very, *very* much, or just . . ."

She never replied. The bell had sounded in mid-sentence, and the girl had run away. Climbing to his proper classroom, Lee handed off the sheets of homework to those as depended upon them and then hurried forward to the teacher's desk to put her things in better order. He was so tired of seeing her fuddling with her papers, untidy piles always in peril of dropping to the floor. Today, Mattie Lou was wearing a sweater he hadn't seen before, a bright red piece of apparel that sorted well with her. He questioned whether he should complement her on it, recollecting just in time that she was one of those who despised the sight of him. Cecil today was in a pair of boots that also Lee hadn't seen before, an expensive looking set with silver chains that chimed with every move. Most of the others were in their usual gear—shoes, shirts, and the girl in back who had forgotten to take off her earmuffs.

She arrived, the teacher, and after blundering about for the desk, found it in its accustomed place. When it came to mathematics, she never called on the same person twice, a pattern that allowed a person a good deal of freedom once he had answered. Taking advantage of it, Lee arose slowly, left the room, and dashed for the boys' room where, somehow, Cecil and two others had arrived there before him. He knew nothing about dice, Lee; he could, however, see that Cecil had put together a hoard of nickels and pennies that was higher by far than the average person's there.

"Cecil?"

"Hm?"

"Who's winning?"

Getting no answer, he went and, while trying to use the urinal at the far end, read the message inscribed in blue-green chalk:

Please do *not* throw your cigarette butts in the toilet. It makes them soggy and hard to light.

Having failed to urinate, he then stood back and surveyed the pornographic frieze that adorned one whole wall, a brilliantly conceived work drawn with much labor by someone who must have known about such things. Craig came in, but then turned and went out again when he saw the place was crowded. Once, just once, Lee would have liked to play poker or dice with these people so that later on he could look back upon it as a fulfillment of his promise to have tried all things before he died.

"Cecil?"

"Hm?"

"Can you lend me a dime?"

The boy didn't answer at first.

"So I can play, too?"

"Hell, no."

"How come!"

"'Cause. We don't want you to go bad on us."

"I've already gone!"

"Naw, you hadn't." He rolled the dice. "You can't go bad till you've had a hundert licks."

"I had twenty-five."

"Look, I don't care if you lie to other people, but now we're talking about me. Anyway, shut up."

He abandoned the place. The hall was long and dark and displayed dozens of framed portraits of some of the town's old-time dignitaries, men in beards, many of them. Sometimes he thought he might encounter the girl who had kissed him on the bus, or on the lips rather, but in truth he wasn't certain he would have recognized her in sunlight. Life was long and dark, and for all he knew the girl had moved on by now to another town and was kissing someone else. Forewarned by an incipient headache gathering force in the amygdala region of the brain, he could predict a two- or three-day spell of black depression heading his way.

Things were not much better when he returned to his desk and found a folded note waiting by his inkwell. It was seldom that he received such notes; indeed, this was just the second that had ever come his way. Putting on a bored expression, he slowly unfolded the thing, but then seemed to lose interest before half finished with it.

"Aren't you even going to read it!" Sonya hissed at him.

Lee yawned. Winter it was, the weather bad, windows closed, and yet far away, he could still hear the same dog calling down from the encompassing hills.

"Hey, Lee!"

"Hm?" (It surprised and disappointed him that Charlie T. would actually come and sit at the same desk with him, a space almost too narrow for one person alone.)

"You stolt anything lately?"

"No. But I've been thinking about it."

"Lookie here." He took out a brightly-colored fan of some nature and opened it, exposing a painting of a woman in a kimono.

"Whew."

"You still going with that girl?"

"What girl?"

The boy thought about it but failed to come up with anyone. Lee waited for him to go away; instead he drew out an Almond Joy candy bar and took off the wrapper.

"Did you steal that one, too?"

"Well, hell, yeah, I stolt it! You don't think I'm going to pay good money for things, do you?"

"No, no."

"Shit, I'll still be here stealing things while you're off to colledge."

Lee had to laugh. "I'll never go to college."

"The shit. What does your old man do?"

"He's an engineer. Electrical."

"Well, shit, he must have all kinds of money!"

There might be something in what the boy had said. "Yeah, but I'm not going to live long enough to be going to college."

"How come?"

"Liver."

"Oh yeah, I heard about that. I had a cousin that died."

The world was full of cousins, many of them dead. Thinking forward to the moment, Lee tried to forestall the tears from gathering.

He waited until 12:17 to finish with the note, and by this time he was at his usual place in the Canteen with Cecil on one side, his Orange Drink on the other, and the Navy veteran called Travis sitting just across from them. The message, telling of how Naomi had become interested in him, was brief, and he was able to go through it repeatedly in no time at all.

"Okay, what does it say?"

Lee shrugged and put on a bored expression. "Some girl," he said. "Claims she likes me."

"Which girl?"

"Shit," said the veteran. "These girls aren't even bleeding yet. Can't see why y'all get so worked up about them."

Lee could feel his gorge rising. There were at least a half-dozen high school girls in that place, and he doubted that a single day could go by without at least one of them bleeding.

"What girl?" Cecil asked again. He was smoking more frequently than herebefore, and had perforce developed a style of doing so in which one would not immediately perceive the cigarette itself, which he kept in darkness just below the level of the table.

"Naomi," Lee said.

"Nothing wrong with that."

"Yeah, but . . . !"

"Calm down."

". . . she used to go with Willard!"

"That don't matter. He didn't do anything to her."

"How do you know?"

"She told me."

"*When* did she tell you?"

"Back when I was going with her."

Lee groaned and put his head down. The music was playing "If," a new song that already he ranked among his top four or five. And then, too, the lights had been turned down very low, giving prominence to a large but not very plentifully adorned Christmas tree standing just next to the jukebox. The mixture of those colors, blue, green, yellow, etcetera, had set up a mysterious ambiance of his favorite kind in which half a dozen couples were dancing in the dark. Looking forward, he could easily envision himself hanging around bars and taverns, a burnt-out case for the rest of his life. And that, of course, was when the school's disciplinary proctor came and put his hand on Leland's shoulder. Sometimes he wished he were more like Cecil, whom the authorities no longer bothered to monitor anymore.

"Sloan!" the man said. "Occurred to me you might be here. You have no idea how much we've been missing you over at the cafeteria."

"I was just fixing to leave."

"Well, let me help."

Forfeiting his Orange Drink, Lee grabbed for his cheeseburger and managed to get it under control. He then let himself be pulled into the standing position and, amid the laughter, prodded toward the door. He had forgotten how bright the Sun could be, especially in holy season.

He looked tired, wan, gaunt, and more sepulchral than ever, Mr. Debardeleben did.

"What'cha reading these days?" he asked, once Lee had entered and taken up a seat on the red leather couch that formed the most luxurious furniture the room contained. "Or have you?"

"Aw, I've been reading about this guy who hunts crocodiles, and he . . ."

"We've already been through that, Lee. Many times! And you led me to believe that you would begin visiting our library more often. It's a good library, Lee, full of *all manner* of stuff."

He looked down. "Yes, sir." He had thought about the library several times.

"Instead you prefer to collaborate with these people. I've spoken with your father—just thought you might want to know."

"Yes, sir; I always want to know."

"Lee, Lee, Lee. Aren't there any attractive girls in your

own neighborhood?"

"There's two."

The man was a melancholy type. Not without compassion, Lee watched as he strode to his cabinet and selected one of his lesser paddles, a narrow affair with not much more threat to it than if it had been an ordinary yardstick of the sort found in hardware and/or clothing stores. He looked for but could not identify the remains of the paddle that Clarence was said to have broken into parts. Going to the center of the room, Sloan now put himself into position and waited for the strokes, two of them, neither with any real force behind it. Putting on an agonized face, he came near to tumbling forward to the floor.

"Now Lee, I want you to *keep away from* that god-awful place, you hear?"

"Yes, sir."

"Or at least until next year."

"Be dead by then."

"You should be." Suddenly he stepped forward to his bookcase and plucked out a thin volume in brown covers. Lee saw at once that he would have been able to read a book like that if he had to, as thin as it was.

"Read it."

"Yes, sir."

"This fellow has the real lowdown. He knows, Lee, he knows what's happening to our beautiful country. Not just Yankees, Lee; we got our own *Southern capitulationists* kowtowing to the Union rag."

"I know it," said Lee, consuming the last of the cheeseburger. "When did you tell him?"

"What?"

"My father."

"Oh, I see him from time to time. But the main thing is, when are you going to start showing us what you can do?" (He didn't know about the girl on the bus.)

"I'm going to start studying real hard."

"May be too late. I don't know, Lee, I look at you, and I see a person who . . ." (He waved his arm about in the air, as if trying to capture one of those December moths that like to get inside doorknobs and keep people awake at night.) "It's a problem."

They studied it together, the problem that had brought Lee to this place. The room was dark and deep, yet not so deep nor dark that they couldn't both detect the sounds of 1950 (girls and motorcycles) leaching through the bricks.

Eight

He hurried straight home and got into the car, waiting for his parents to set out on this year's tour of the town's Christmas decorations. They were genteel people and mild, easily pleased, who worked hard and asked for little. Sitting just behind his father, he inspected the back of his head, or at any rate that part of it not hidden by his hat. His hair was twenty percent grey by now, and his nose, like those of all the family in the male line, was a salient thing, as big and blunt as a parsnip almost. One could not see his eyes of course, which remained all times deep within the shadows established by the brim of his brown felt hat. This man had had adventures—that much had been revealed in family discussions—but as to what those episodes had consisted in . . . Lee didn't know.

Next, his mother, a dignified woman dressed in the clothes she used each year at this time for viewing Christmas decorations. She had descended from European royalty, one would have thought, instead of the Alabama mail carrier and part-time farmer who comprised Leland's actual grandfather. Looking at her from the other side, Lee descried the uncontrollable shock of dense black hair she had passed to her elder son. Many other qualities she had gifted him as well, some good, some of neutral value, and one or two others as well.

Lee's attention now turned to his brother, a pale quantity who loved to ride stretched out on that shelf between the back seat and rear window. Here the boy could sleep if need be, or scrutinize the night sky, or present an amusing sight to people in other cars. And then, too, he gloried in that hypnogogic state that brought perfect peace without at the same time entraining the disadvantages of death. He also carried an army canteen full of lemonade and liked to drink from it while in the prone position.

The dog came, too. Turning to look one another in the face, Lee was reminded that he never had and most likely never would be able to communicate with this creature across the man-dog divide that had led to so many misunderstandings in the past. Each thought the other insane. Bright lights and Christmas trees meant nothing to so rudimentary an animal, whose brain couldn't have been even as large as its container.

They went direct to where the quality dwelled and drove past slowly, actually stopping in front of a two-story home with a brilliantly-illuminated tree set up on the balcony. The householder could have done even better than that, had he so wanted—he was Superintendent of Education for the entire county. Came next an array of little elves jumping up and down in front of the place where Milton Evans lived; here Leland's father delayed for a long time, entranced with it, apparently. Two doors further there was a manger scene with three wise persons, one of them a negro or near it, peering into a rude-looking crib whose contents could not be identified from the street.

There were other displays, all of them worth seeing. If he had his way, Leland, the city would be similarly lit up all through the year, either that or infested with garish manifestations of neon from evening to dawn.

The middle-class people had done almost as well, although sometimes one came upon places where last year's display had been replicated without changes. At the corner of 10th and Highland they found a home with perhaps the paltriest wreath ever seen, a diseased-looking artifact hung crookedly at the door. Leland's father stopped and looked at it for a long time, saying nothing. Lee was not surprised to see that some of the most wretched dwellings, mere trailers in some cases, had gone to the greatest lengths. (They were in a bad neighborhood now, and Leland's father had no interest in slowing down.) Some of these people had actually collaborated to join their homes together in strings of light. It tended to confirm Lee's old-time suspicion that poverty had its attractions.

Thus Lee and thus his family, and by 8:15 the inspection was over. Arriving back at home, he eschewed his second-favorite radio program and instead hurried into his best clothes. He might attend any number of dances during the course of a month, but none bore comparison with what took place December 23rd each year.

Looking neither to left nor yet to right, he ran to school in under six minutes and entered with a bored expression. His suit was blue, and there was a flower pinned to his lapel. Furthermore, the place was as dark as he liked, and although it wasn't "My Foolish Heart" they were playing, the music was adequate, too. Right away he saw Cecil dancing with Gwen and doing it in such a way as that they looked like a single person of unnatural size. As to Charlie T., Lee had never seen him in a suit, or even normal clothes for that matter. He carried two bunches of flowers, one in each hand.

"Hey, how come you got *two* bunches?" Lee asked.

"In case the first one don't work," said he, holding up what looked to Lee like a spray of daffodils. (The other hand held roses.)

"Well, who are they for?"

The boy indicated vaguely toward the girls at large, a considerable array of seventh-, eighth-, and ninth-graders in well-shod shoes and evening dresses. Some detested the sight of him, some didn't, and some were potential wives of his. He focused in upon an older girl in brown velvet whom at first Lee suspected of having been the girl on the bus. (She wasn't.) He then waved to Mildred Weston, who actually looked rather good tonight despite herself. She had removed her glasses and put them away where she would no doubt take them out again when the night was done. But she did not wave back.

He entertained no hope that he might meet up with the high school girl who had molested him in the Canteen—she would be attending other parties this season, older ones where he himself had no chance of an invitation. Thinking of her, his mind began to drift, drifting back to *her* and to the strange affiliation he seemed to have with older girls. He turned to watch one of the chaperons, a thirty- or forty-year-old woman who had preserved at least some portion of her quondam appeal, as he called it. To kiss a woman of that kind he would need a chair or ladder, and even then would have to stand on tiptoes. He didn't want that, not with a woman whose upper arms were as heavy as hers and in addition bore a vaccination mark.

He had avoided all thought of Naomi, even though three several persons, friends of hers, had advised him she'd be here. That was when the music shifted over to one of the better songs of that year, a Mel Tormé production that ranked among the best. Slowly and slowly he could feel himself softening and romanticizing, the inexorable result on him of music, darkness, and girls in pastel dresses. They comprised, those people, a phantasmagoric scene, so much so that he strove to ward off one of his most constant and unwanted thoughts, namely that in days to come they'd all have turned into a few hundred bones scattered about at large. His future wife, was she among that group? No, probably not, not as long as none of them had that high forehead and unique expression of the face that he required in wives of his.

Naomi also was wearing an iridescent gown of some description, a multi-colored garment that compared and contrasted her with a certain species of dragonfly. Pretty soon he'd have to go to her and make an utterance, a friendly remark, or something to make her laugh. Thinking about it (and going over his inventory of witticisms), he strolled to the punchbowl and ladled himself a full steeping glass of a bark-colored fluid that had lemons floating in it. He knew nothing of "steeping" in other contexts and therefore now put this down also into that other inventory of his, his list of words. Cecil, he saw, had migrated over toward the Christmas tree and had engaged himself in what either was an argument with Gwen or else an enactment of passion coming to the surface at just this time. On the other hand, his friend Smitty was still holding to his flowers, yellow ones and red.

He had been waiting for "My Foolish Heart" as sung by Billy Eckstine, hoping to exploit it as the backdrop for his approach to Naomi and the two or three friends grouped protectively around her; so much the greater, then, was his disappointment when instead of serious music, an inane little tune came on, a cheerful business representing the most negative aspect of 1950. Let the world be romantic and dark, let it make Lee tremble, or let there be no world at all! Steve came up.

"I didn't know if you was coming tonight," he stated.

"Yeah."

"Because of Naomi?"

And so that was it; even Steve knew more about his affairs than did Lee himself.

"I guess."

"She's not so bad. I took her to the movies couple of years ago."

"Which movie?"

"You better go talk to her. She's waiting."

"Yeah."

"When?"

Lee pushed off. As he drew nearer to her (and further from the wall) his vision improved, and he could see that she was wearing a little tiara of some sort, a preposterous appliance that had slipped off to one side. He had not yet come up with any kind of witticism, and by this time he had hardly three seconds to find one. Still furrowing through his inventory, he went and stood just next to her in such a way as that both of them could view the dance floor in its entirety.

She was shorter than Lee, and he gave thanks for that. Glancing peripherally at her, he could see the outer perimeter of her translucent eyeball, a convex gel of about the size of his own such organ. Ten seconds having passed, her perfume, which was of a certain wavelength, reached him where he stood. Generally, Lee preferred woodland smells—lavender and rue—but he found hers quite as good. (Next to lavender and rue, he liked honeysuckle, magnolia, and gardenia respectively, and in that order.)

"Hi," he said, turning upon her without premeditation, causing her to jump back two inches. He yawned. "I wasn't sure whether I'd come tonight or not."

She continued to look straight forward, her vision fixed upon a certain spot. Across the way Steve was urging him on with hand signals, a series of movements that Lee soon gave up trying to interpret.

"When are they going to hand out the presents? Naw, I was just wondering."

Now she turned. It was the first time he had seen her at that range, and he had only a moment to make his appraisal before he'd have to speak again, or look away, or take out a cigarette. In that brief time he saw a good deal of what her appearance looked like, and what he saw looked all right to him. Putting aside her nose and perhaps chin, she was a reasonable person, and well-matched with Lee at Lee's current developmental stage. He was taller than she.

"Cecil and me, we were over to the Canteen yesterday."

"Yes, and got into trouble, too. That's what Jean said."

"Oh, good Lord. I don't care about stuff like that anymore! I'm used to it."

Never had he seen such admiration in the eyes of a female standing face-to-face with him. All previous experiences with women now faded into things that were small and far away.

"Yeah, we don't even notice it anymore."

The girl came closer. Her perfume *might* have some magnolia in it, a little bit.

"Want to dance? Naw, you don't have to."

He led her out to the center of the floor and put his hand, first, on two or three ribs on this side and then, secondly, the other side. He reckoned her as of about twenty pounds lighter than the high school girl who had assaulted him in October. He did not know, Lee, the size of the girl on the bus. In the meantime, a piece of decent music had just come on. Together with the dark and the surrounding vision of his friends, of presents heaped up under the tree, and Tony Bennett, he was in real peril of falling in love four or five years too early.

They danced three dances in quick succession and then went off to one side in order to talk about it. She was not as pretty as Gwen, nor yet even as Sonya with her milk-colored hair; she was, however, a better-looking human being than some. And then, too, her father was a carpenter and a part-timer roofer, occupations that served a more indisputable need than some he could have mentioned.

The floor was crowded by now, and the music had settled into a song cycle by Patti Page, Jo Stafford, and the

rest of that school. Suddenly he locked eyes with Mr. Debardeleben, a bleak figure who had taken up in the exact
center of the room. There was very little that man failed to
see, not excluding Leland and the mediocre-looking girl
sitting just across from him. Putting on a boyish smile, Lee
threw up his hand and waved at him enthusiastically, getting absolutely nothing in return. Meantime the girl's
hand lay at random on the table, where Lee could see that
she had suffered from a broken finger at some juncture,
leaving the thing askew at that particular place. She removed her hand from sight and positioned it under the
other.

"Naw, it's alright," Lee said. "Heck, I had a broken leg
when I was nine."

"Did it hurt?"

"I guess. But I don't pay attention to stuff like that anymore."

She came nearer. There was now no question but that
Cecil and Gwen had gotten into a disagreement of some
sort. He hated to see it—the two of them standing ten feet
apart and staring hotly at each other. For one brief moment there came to him the unworthy notion that perhaps he could pick up with her where Cecil had left off, an
impossibility if ever any was. Suddenly, out of nowhere,
"Now and Then There's a Fool Such as I" came on. Taking
Naomi by the wrist, he pulled her to her feet and to the
edge of the floor, where they danced together happily for
the next three minutes. Such moments were so rare, a
mere hour or two out of an entire month. It pointed to the
essential unfairness of things and his recurring theory that
life was a "two percent solution," so to speak, and the rest
all misery and waste. A thousand years might go by, and
still he'd be waiting to hear that particular song again.

"We're going to visit my grandmother next week," Lee
mentioned after they had gone back, and the girl had again
left her bent finger in view. "We'll probably go fishing, too."

"*We* went fishing one time."

"Good." Gwen had disappeared into the girls' facility. Where was Cecil? Lee found him at last dancing with Margaret Bunting, the one single girl in Alabama who could have stood up to Gwen in terms of beauty and prestige. Lee yawned and, after pushing his punch off to one side, stood and strode halfway across the floor before returning and apologizing.

"I need to see somebody," he explained. "But I'm coming right back."

She agreed to it. The music was over, and he was able to find Cecil before the next record began.

"What happened?" he asked somewhat belligerently.

"Hm?"

"Gwen!"

"She has her way of doing things, and I have mine."

"Yeah, but . . . !"

"Just calm down, okay? Hey, I don't stick my nose into *your* business, do I?"

"I don't have any business! Besides, I . . ."

"Anyway, shut up. What, you don't like Margaret?" He nudged Margaret to the fore, allowing Lee to gaze upon her. Dressed as she was in a white gown that set off the residues of last summer's suntan, she was a vision that seemed to have sprung fully formed out of angel food cake. He could not but offer to shake with her.

"Hi."

She laughed. She was of his own precise height, but not comparable to him in other ways. More than that, she seemed to have a bust that drew his vision against his will. Her hand, too, was white, and had the tiniest little ring on it, holding a pale green stone.

"Cecil and me, we sit next to each other," Lee described. "Because of the alphabet."

She drew back and laughed out loud at him. God, she was pretty. To be laughed at, really that was about all he could expect at that particular time in connection with girls like that. He had always known, of course, that Gwen wouldn't last. And then, too, this "Margaret" had wider hips and was better set-up for the duties of a wife.

The space now had seventeen couples on the floor, some of them dancing with consummate skill. They had heard perhaps thirty pieces of music by now, among them some of the finest art products of 1950. His opinion of the chaperone, who generally ignored them, had also improved. The punch, too, was good, pretty good, even if the quality had begun to peter out as the level fell lower and the molten ice rendered the stuff less lemony than Lee would have preferred. It angered him further when the music stopped, the lights came on, and the students began to gather about the tree.

Itself, the tree was ornamented with "angel's hair" (so-called) that made him think of Margaret and Gwen. And yet the angel itself, a plastic item sitting atop the tree, was an ordinary blond with stumpy wings. Turning next to the gifts, a cantilevered hill of square and rectangular objects wrapped in papers of various sorts, he could feel himself growing more excited than was good for him. "Calm down!" he said to himself. "Easy now, just calm down, that's right." It was an anomaly, that his system still worked in such childish ways. Putting on a tired face, he walked off a distance, came back, and then waited about with his hands in his pockets while Mildred Weston, slowly and with an annoyed look (she was wearing her glasses now), unwrapped the gift given her by the unrevealed person who had drawn her name. It was, of course, a book.

"Thank you," she said to the crowd at large. A slight applause followed. Had she read that particular book already? Very likely, judging from her face. Came next Acedia, the most corpulent girl in town, who had been given a bottle of perfume large enough to suffice her for a very long time. Applause followed.

"Shit!" said Smitty in low voice. "She won't have to take no baths anymore! What is that, formaldehyde?"

Mr. Debardeleben had also been given a present, a large object wrapped in blue which he preferred to set on the floor. He mistrusted it, Lee divined.

Three or four other presents were unwrapped, the usual things for the most part, which is to say until Cecil's turn came about. Putting his cigarette in the corner of his mouth, he quickly and efficiently unwrapped a box of shotgun shells, a logical gift for a person who already owned the pertinent weapon. Lee saw that his own gift of a billfold (destined for Earl Clechum) was near to the surface of the pile—he had wrapped it himself and placed it there. Picking daintily at the bow, the recipient proceeded to unwrap the thing with the most extravagant care, as if he might be more interested in the paper with the picture of the North Pole on it than in the gift itself.

"Get on with it!" Lloyd called out in loud voice. And yet the fellow continued with his tedious method. He had managed to save a good eighteen inches of glossy ribbon.

"A billfold! A palpable billfold!"

Lee blushed. Stolen at great risk from a well-known entrepot on Noble Street, he could feel himself becoming more like Clarence every day.

"Hope you like it," he said. "It wasn't easy."

Naomi tugged at his sleeve. "You're not supposed to tell who bought it."

"I didn't! Buy it, I mean."

Came next Smitty himself, who had been given a set of toy plastic handcuffs—the whole room burst out laughing—toy plastic handcuffs that cost perhaps a quarter at the downtown Woolworth's store. He was hurt by that gift, as Lee was surprised to see.

"Shit. There waddn't no call for that."

Came then the teacher's turn. She was a confused and hapless individual with thick glasses that incorporated a great deal of fog in the prescription. Older than she should have been and with a voice like a crow's, she was the most beloved woman in town. And yet some miscreant had actually given her a pair of panties about five sizes too large.

"Good Lord."

Impossible not to laugh, even those who didn't want to.

"That's not nice!" Naomi said. (Already Lee was getting tired of this person.) "Gollee!"

The woman gathered them up and looked at them. Lee knew about the salaries of school teachers, and it occurred to him she might find a use for them after all. Applause followed.

His own gift came due at just past nine o'clock. Screwing himself up for the hilarity that he expected, he unwrapped the thing quickly and held it up for all to see. He had learned long ago to meet personal abuses head-on and be done with them at once.

They danced till ten, at which point the lights came back on. Cecil was going with Margaret now, and Gwen no longer was present. Looking back upon it from later on, the next he remembered he was waiting on the curb for Naomi's parents to come and gather her up. He expected to be treated in a welcoming fashion by these people who no doubt had heard by now that his father was an electrical engineer.

"You'll have to come visit us sometime," the woman said, smiling maternally. "We always like to see Naomi's friends."

Lee smiled boyishly and shook with the old man, a rough-looking personage who appeared to be embarrassed by the situation.

"You betcha," he said, and drove away. His head looked like a box when seen from the rear, and had ears on it as big as human hands. Lee turned toward home. A pretty good chapter, it seemed to him, in which he had both carried out his first date, had learnt that Gwen was available, and had collected this year's most outrageous gift.

Nine

Already he had seen at least one car with a Georgia and another with a Connecticut (it made his gorge rise) plate on it. The country was drawing together—he hated it—and soon one location would be like any other. That was when they came into a town and almost at once exited out the other side, leaving Lee with the memory of a blue hound lying half in the road and half in someone's yard. It was still the South, he knew it for a certainty when they passed an aged negro in overalls hobbling down along the highway toward no conceivable destination. The land was cursed. God, he loved it.

Next, he turned his notice upon his father's head, a cubic manifestation mostly hidden beneath the brim of his crumpled hat. That hat sustained memories and much pessimism, enough to have pointed his children in the same direction. And in short, he was a wistful man with large pores in his nose. Next, he turned, Lee, to his mother, trying with but little success to guess *her* theories, *her* loves and past. Just then a large blue bat swooped down and glanced into the Chevrolet itself. The news came on. Lee's father disliked hearing these matters reported in a woman's (Pauline Frederick's) voice, which tended to palliate matters and rob them of seriousness. He endured it for perhaps three seconds and then began tampering with the dial in a search for something better.

The dashboard had lights on it—green ones, two that were red, and his favorite, pale blue, that mixed perfectly, both with his own personality and the outside black night that had come down around them. To push that darkness off to one side and continue forward required a car with broad sails, maps, visible stars, and perfect coordination on the part of the pilot.

They possessed all of these, and by the time they had run past Wetumpka, his brother had gone to sleep. His father was *not* asleep, as Lee could determine by the glow of his cigarette, for upon *him* had fallen the responsibility of everything, including money, a thermos of coffee, and a jar to pee in. Soon now his mother would begin singing, a habit of hers when the family was together and going somewhere. Lee would remember this. Meantime the ash on Poor Albert's cigarette had grown so long and tenuous that Lee expected momentarily to see it collapse into his lap. True, the man had a talent for ashes of impossible length. That was when Lee's mother began singing his first-favorite nighttime traveling song:

> No one here can love or understand me,
> Oh what hard-luck stories they all hand me.
> Make my bed and light the light,
> I'll arrive late tonight
> Blackbird, bye, bye.

There was no question but that she sang well. And no question but that this song, that blended so well with Alabama and the night, with occasional filling stations and faraway homes with feeble lights burning in them, with cicadas and bats, the patched Moon, vigilant mules, and here and there a column of exhausted ungulates wending homeward in single file, of volcanoes exuding a lava as green as grass, radio towers, of grunting hogs, the dog and Lee and . . . And that was when the ash fell into his father's lap.

They left the road and halted long enough to permit the man to beat out the sparks that had set his pants on fire. Too, he had brought a small flask of whiskey with him that fitted ideally into his vest pocket on the left-hand side. He liked to sip at it from time to time to enhance his driving. Strolling further down the roadbed, he then opened those same pants and "took a leak," as generally he called it. Lee's mother had meantime alternated over into one of the songs that must have been popular when she was young and when a family's livestock was the best thing they had:

Go and tell Aunt Rhody
the old grey goose is dead,
the one she's been saving
to make a feather bed.

Pleased by the music, Lee's brother had come awake to listen to it. There were four of them in that car, and the rest of the world might well be extinct for all that Lee could care. Continuing in that line of thought, he speculated on the corpses, the starved dogs, unanswered telephones, and department stores when in an unpopulated world everything would be free of charge. "Good Lord," said Leland to himself, "that's a strange thing to wish for, a boy my age."

Truth was, he hungered for earthquakes, thunder and lightning, and great wars, followed up by a renewal of a Dark Ages even more tenebrous than the last one. He wished for other things too, a submarine for example, or a hot-air balloon. Wanted a farm of his own and then, last of all, to set foot on the uncanny surface of Uranus, his favorite of the greater planets. Wanted numerous girls, the cream of northern Alabama, and to see his name made famous throughout the South. Not that he expected all of it at once! No, he was still quite young as yet, and could tarry for a certain while.

It was about as dark as ever he had seen it, which is to say until he realized that he had been dreaming. Forcing open first one lid and then another, he climbed to the window and examined the outside world. In the meantime a wind had come up, and it appeared to him as if the night had turned into a viscous material swirling back and forth. His father, certainly, had not changed, and Lee was able with his methods to ascertain that he was still awake. Perhaps they had lost the way, perhaps not, but in neither case would Lee have wished to call attention to the fact. They were moving deeper into the night. The latitudinous Moon had come to rest in an unfrequented place, whileas the stars, worn down by now to the merest things, were on the verge of going out. He could have scooped up the whole number of them in an average-size mason jar.

He was interested equally in signs. They passed a billboard with the picture of a beautiful woman on it (smoking a cigarette) who reminded him in some ways of Gwen, and in others of a particular eleventh-grader whose name he didn't yet know. He next turned his notice to a bejeweled traffic sign telling of danger up ahead. They ran over a railway track, making haste lest a train arrive suddenly. He spotted a half-dozen swamp niggers, as these were called, pilgrimaging southwardly down the shoulder of the road.

A thousand years might go by, but never would Lee understand why people had chosen to sleep at night instead of the other way around. His nervousness increased, and probably he should have swallowed one of his pharmaceuticals at this juncture. The dog meantime had lapsed off into perturbed dreams, while his brother had fallen fully unconscious on his ledge. He even believed that his mother might be sleeping, too, until he heard her singing in a somewhat diminished voice:

Stars and steel guitars
And luscious lips as red as wine
Stole somebody's heart

And I'm afraid that it was mine.

The words pushed aside the rubbish that cluttered Leland's mind and would remain forever there, though another thousand years go by.

His father was *not* unconscious, and by the time they came into the outlying suburbs—two shacks and a filling station—of the little river town his grandfather had founded, Lee was so nearly asleep himself that he had to be roused by one of the adults. His assignment was to find his way up to the front porch of William's House and knock on the door, a stunt that was supposed to surprise and delight his ancient grandmother. He was accustomed to it, being put to use that way and made an agent of his father's tricks.

He had seen this place before, an unpainted structure with all sorts of stained glass and fancy fretwork running around the architrave. Stumbling up the stairs, he went and took up a position on the porch, surprised that the woman was still on vigil at one o'clock in the morning. They looked at each other warily through the frosted glass.

"Hi!" Lee said.

No sound came to him from within the enormous building.

"It's just me," he added.

Across the road, two lights came on in the neighbor's house. Somewhere a dog was barking. From inside he could hear the sort of footsteps that he associated with old people who have become humpbacked from age and inclination. A lamp came on, a kerosene lantern to reckon from the granular character of the haze. From neighboring houses, two dogs were coming from opposite directions. Lee was surprised to have the rooster crowing at this untoward hour, a violation of its usual routine. No doubt his father would be grinning at all this, just the thing to finish off a perfect day.

"Ga-ga?" (It was his old-time expression, "Ga-ga," for his grandmother.)

"What do you mean out there on my front porch!"

"Nothing."

A long silence intervened. The bravest of the dogs had come forward and was interrogating Leland's purpose with his nose. And then: "Is Young Albert out there?"

"No, ma'am! He's in the car."

She went around, moving slowly, and opened the curtain, giving her a pretty good vantage on Young Albert's Ford. Lee, confident it would happen, waited for her to return to the door.

"Well," she said. "I reckon it's alright."

She opened the door an inch or two, enough to let Lee see the .32 caliber semi-automatic trembling in her hand.

"Hi!" Lee said.

She was a tentative sort of person and had some trouble bending low enough to make out his identity.

"Looks like . . ."

"Yes, ma'am."

"Albert's boy."

"Yes, ma'am. Can we come in?"

The dog, the brave one, had entered already, and was sniffing at Lee's and his grandmother's four shoes and feet. Came now Leland's people—a groggy brother and two adults. His father was grinning broadly. His mother, on the other hand, was faded-looking and was bringing two pieces of small luggage. Lee was pleased the old woman had set up a Christmas tree, however small. And yet she must have possessed ten thousand trees better than this one among the some two hundred and forty acres still pertaining to her.

They gathered in the parlor and began passing compliments back and forth. Uncanny, how the old time smells still lingered here, essence of camphor and linseed oil, cakes, lavender, and pies. A thousand years might go by. His eye, Lee's, traveled by habit to the massy portrait on the wall of his entombed grandfather, a stern man, rectitudinous, afflicted with no tolerance whatsoever—just the sort that later on Lee was to become and adore. That portrait hung just above an antique clock of high value, a thing as big as some of the biggest clocks normally seen. Enchanted by these old familiar artifacts, not to mention the shotgun in the corner and calendar on the wall with the picture of Jeff Davis on it, Lee went and looked down the long dark corridor that had intrigued and worried him for so long. He could discern pieces of large furniture that lined the hallway, also a blistered mirror that had mostly peeled away by now. The house and its features had been assembled in 1898, but Lee did not have enough history to visualize the world of that day, when people like his grandfather had held sway.

He was pointed to the bedroom, shown his pajamas, and ordered into bed. His brother was mostly still asleep for hours, and their father was able to lift him up and lay him down next to the recumbent Leland, an embryo in a vitelline skein. His eyelids, unfortunately, were translucent, and the boy could witness all that happened during the course of nights. Even more annoying were the adults, who continued to gossip in the next room, the three of them excitedly exchanging banalities not worth hearing. His grandmother's voice tended to peter out at the end of sentences, but he could get the gist of it. Twice she chuckled. "Heh, heh."

Thus Lee—it was one o'clock in the morning, he could hear an owl blaring from not very far away. He was in the very room (he tried to picture it) in which his father had been conceived. Ten thousand years might go by, and forever there'd be additional Peflies emerging into life. A house and home, a dog and car, pictures on the wall— seldom had he felt snugger and/or smug than at just this time. Smacking his lips over it, he fell asleep and stayed that way until about two hours later, when he awoke to see . . .

. . . his father down on one knee in front of the hearth. The man had brought together some dozen lengths of hardwood and was using three or four several pinecones to kindle a fire. No doubt he imagined himself the only one awake, wherefore Lee took care to maintain perfect silence. From far away came the sound of a train full of Alabamians running at full speed through the counties and, nearer at hand, the owl giving one last call that would have to suffice him for the rest of the night.

His father was a wistful man, and his head was square. From his position, Lee was actually able to look through a slice of the man's glasses, which gave a sharp and well-defined view of things as viewed by an engineer. Lee knew nothing of the experiences that had made him as melancholy as he was, nor of the problems which he was wont to keep to himself. Lee didn't even know much about his work, except that it entailed the making of blueprints and required a lot of time. Further still, Lee wasn't exactly sure of his own position in the family and whether he was growing up in accord with the plans that the man had blueprinted for *him*. But he had been wrong, Lee, about the owl, who now blared one additional time that really did turn out to be the last of the night.

Ten

He awoke unto an antique world. The washbowl had water in it, the smell of breakfast filled the house, and his brother was gone. Leaping to shirt and trousers, he strode quickly to the kitchen, where the family had met already and already was half through the dumplings and eggs. Lee saluted them and grinned boyishly, confident that his grandmother and uncle would greet him in the amazed and congratulatory way that he had come to expect.

"Good gracious alive! That can't be Lee, can it?" (His voice was faint and came as if from far away.)

"Yes, sir; it is."

"Well, come on over here, for goodness sakes, and get some waffles afore they're all gone."

Lee consented to it. His brother had consumed several of the things already, as could be seen in the fluid molasses draining from his chin. Lee settled across from his father who, still in robe and slippers, appeared to be reading the local newspaper. He was happy here, here in William's House, and the ash on his cigarette was longer, too. Lee reached tentatively for a waffle, drew it to himself, and covered it, not in syrup this time, but rather the brown honey still regularly vouchsafed them by his extinct grandfather's well-trained bees. He was also to remember, Lee, a certain little pink dish divided into compartments, each chamber holding a separate kind of jam and jelly and watermelon rind pickle. Further, there was a jar of strawberry preserves which they used with reserve. Coffee—he wasn't allowed any. Nor any of the scuppernong wine that sat on a shelf of its own just below the massy portrait of his grandmother's father, a bearded man who had slain his meed of trespassing northerners all those years ago.

It was a bright winter day, doves flying over, the scent of parched peanuts coming from the kitchen. He was both anxious to get outside, Lee, but anxious also to stay with these older people telling stories of the most remote times, when fog and smoke covered most of Alabama. Especially he admired his uncle, a hale man who had been delivering the mails for thirty years and was acknowledged the best fisherman in the county. His voice, however, was extraordinarily soft, even by local standards, and Lee had to bend close to pick up his words. He had a straw hat that he wore throughout the day, but his neck and face were sunburned just the same.

"Good gracious alive," he said.

Lee came nearer.

"What you boys been doing?"

"Nothing," said Lee. "Went to Tuscaloosa."

"Did!"

"Yes, sir. But my reed was broken." (He made no reference to the girl.)

"Well, I'll be jiggered. Done any fishing?"

"No, sir. But I sure would like to."

"Me, too," Leland's brother said. "I sure would like to, just as much as he would."

The man laughed. His arms were brawny from having dredged in so many bass, big ones that oftentimes ended up pictured in the newspaper.

"Well. I got to go to Enterprise this morning. But maybe we can do some fishing tonight. Unless you don't want to."

"Sounds like a good idea to me."

"Shoot, sounds good to me, too!"

"Which one does it sound better to?" He laughed a laugh, the man, like a dry breeze sifting through brown stalks of last year's corn. And then, too, he had a grid on the back of his sunburnt neck that looked very like the waffles they had just consumed, the result of too much Sun over too long a time. As fascinated as he was, and as charmed, Lee scarcely noted that his grandmother had also been speaking over the past half-minute in a voice that was nearly as soft as her eldest son's. Lee turned to her now, and they looked at each other. Her eyes must have been oval at one period, but now the lower lid had formed a little spout whence some of the juice had flowed away.

"No," she said. "I don't reckon you-all need to be down to the river in the middle of the night. You never know."

"It'll be all right, mama."

"No. I don't hardly think so." Suddenly she jumped

back, startled to find Leland's brother just next to her. And yet they had been introduced several times before. That was when Leland's uncle rose slowly, stretched, chuckled, rolled a cigarette, and then took out his knife and began paring at his nails. It was exceedingly sharp, that knife, and the blade had worn down over time to a substantial thinness. Lee came nearer to look at it. The man took no great care, apparently, when he micturated, and the front of his trousers bore all kinds of tiny stains. And if his three brothers had all gone off to college and turned into dentists and engineers and the sort, he remained by general consent the wisest of the lot. Suddenly he strode around to Leland's brother, lifted him, left the house, and then began striding off to town with the boy riding on his shoulders.

He had hoped, had Lee, that his father might eventually finish up with the funny papers; instead, the man appeared to have gotten bogged down in *Mutt and Jeff.* Reduced to the obverse of the page, Lee harkened to Alley Oop and his good friend Foozy sitting astride their dinosaur. Later on, looking back upon it, he could not accept the passing away of these people and the apathy they were to receive at the hands of the modern world.

With nothing left to do, no homework or anything of that sort, he opted to go to the barn and feed the chickens, but had no sooner arrived there than the recording machine in his head was captured by the ineffable smell of cotton and hay and compacted manure. The cows and horse had all been given chambers of their own, revealing the excellence in carpentry that had typified his grandfather. He was surrounded here, Leland, by the ghosts of ten thousand animals jostling for space. In the corner he spied an old-time harness rotted down to a mere lump of leather, too heavy for him to lift. What sort of men had these been who had toiled themselves to death with such awkward equipment? Who had understood mules and in turn been understood by them? And who now were abominated for poor dentition and sunburnt necks?

He could feel his gorge rising. The roof had holes in it, and rays of sunshine, each of about an inch in girth, were ricocheting back and forth among the stalls. Probing the nearest of these beams with his finger, Lee tried to stir up the little motes of dust floating in and out of ken. There was more to this than met the eye, more to light and more to dust, and more to a particular style of life.

The chickens were baffled by his appearance, nor did he rightly know how to put them at ease. Seizing one by the neck, he tried to force-feed grain to the creature, which is to say until the foul thing put its spur into the connective tissue between the boy's thumb and finger. He was good at mathematics and pretty good at fishing, but knew nothing of hens, mules, darning needles, and molasses-making. Nor knew he aught about the twenty-foot-high levee that defended the town on three sides.

This county had better than a thousand souls in it, most of them having awakened, having sat about for a time, and having gone back to bed. He did see one elderly woman sitting on her porch in a stationary position, her gaze traveling out over the unfamiliar scenes of youth. Lee turned and bowed sweepingly to her. The windows of her home were hued, and, owing to the imperfect state of glass production in those days, offered an imperfect reflection of either herself or someone sitting on her porch. And was it really true those windows were thicker at the bottom, the material "running downhill," as it were, over the course of years? She also owned a cat, providing her with another system for monitoring the comings and goings of people.

The town was old, and the prevailing philosophy, which happened to be Leland's too, was that death *would* come, and it behooved a person to await it with all the absolute indifference available. He knew, too, that it had been bruited among scientists that someday the *entire world* would end. Taking on a melancholy mien, he hobbled past a three-story home with a gazebo out front and a good-looking, though rural, sort of woman dithering with her flowers. There was no question but that he, descended from a long line of Celto-Teutonic types, was just such a one as to whom these gazebos and goldfish ponds most rightly appertained. And when he died, he wanted to die in a bed in a house in a county that had been settled by his grandfathers.

It was supposed to be winter, but in fact the climate had pretty much come to a stop in October. He had not yet stepped on a single crack, and by the time he arrived at the drugstore, there were three people hovering over the merchandise in there. Expecting to be welcomed warmly, if not exuberantly, he entered recklessly, wearing an impatient face. The woman had aged a few months since last he had seen her, but had remained recognizable even so. She possessed some of the deepest bosoms in Alabama, soft ones that trembled when she spoke.

"No!" she said. "That can't be Lee!"

He argued that he was.

"Well, I declare. Why didn't you come see us?"

"I did."

"Well, that's good. Did you bring your daddy?"

"Aw, they have to go to Enterprise. But we're going fishing tonight, Dana and me."

"No!"

"Yes, ma'am. We are."

"Well, I'll be."

In obedience to her posture, her left breast (his favorite) was raised a little bit higher than her right, and if he looked directly at it, he believed that he could discern the nozzle itself, a raspberry-size epiphenomenon that concluded the gland.

"Could I have a vanilla milkshake?" he inquired uncertainly.

"No, sweetie. But I'll sell you one."

Lee grinned. Now it was the *right* one that was higher. That was when the proprietor, a man who had gone bald from staying indoors so much of the time, came up and poked him in the ribs. "Well, look who's here!"

Lee grinned.

"Where's Young Albert?"

"Aw, he had to go to Enterprise. Dana and me are going fishing."

"Can I come too?"

Lee said nothing. The boat was small enough, and if Dana's negro and Lee's own younger brother were also to come, there'd not be room for all of them. Suddenly he threw up his hand and waved to the pharmacist, glad of the distraction. This was a quiet sort of person who maintained what was perhaps the tidiest and best-organized array of chemicals and lotions that Lee was ever to see. Lee knew two things about this drugstore, about the woman, the pharmacist, and the rest, namely that the milkshake would have two (not one) scoops of ice cream in it and, secondly, that he would not be made to pay. This was chiefly the reason he had not counted the small supply of coins he carried in his vest.

A person could live in a town like this and go fishing every day. Or, a person could grow up and marry a local girl. Of course there'd be no Cecil here, no Gwen nor Canteen nor marching band nor anything of that kind. On the other hand, this town was older and smaller, with no traffic lights, less congestion, and a smaller likelihood that he'd end up in jail.

He finished his milkshake and waited to see if he'd be offered another. Just then his uncle marched past in front of the store with Leland's brother riding on his shoulders. By this time there were at least five persons in town, and although it was an hour before lunchtime, already the place was stirring. Two mule teams were winking at each other across the courthouse square. Meantime the great Methodist bell had begun to toll, producing a noise that easily overwhelmed the other churches. Lee's eye moved to the John Wilkes Booth memorial fountain, where two girls were wading up to their knees in the stuff, a thing not feasible were it *truly* winter.

He made his tour of the square, sometimes stopping to peer into one or another of the shops, especially Charles Creamer's hardware store. Above, two hawks flew over before then grinding down to a halt in midair, intrigued, apparently, by the activity taking place ten thousand feet below. He moved past the three weird negroes sitting on a bench in front of the dry goods store. These people shared a single pair of glasses which they passed back and forth. Lee stopped and stood, waiting with considerable patience to be recognized. The glasses were smudged and one of the lenses was broken. "Well, blow me down! Looks like Poor Albert's boy!"

Lee grinned. The glasses had ended up with the man called "Blue," an aged individual with a history of wives.

"Where you been?"

"Aw, I've been up in ————." (He gave here the name of the town in which he had passed the last eleven years.)

"Have?"

"Yeah. We're going fishing tonight, Dana and me."

"Are?"

"Yeah." He reached for a dime and gave it over to the man, aware that two other hands were outstretched as well. "We're going to set out a trotline."

"Well, I'll be."

But already they were getting bored with him. Lee retrieved the glasses, which had fallen to the ground, and awarded them to the albino called "Half-and-Half." He observed that his uncle had completed his own tour of

town and had turned homeward, followed by Leland's
smaller brother. Apart from these, Lee perceived a white
woman—he knew her—doing her Friday marketing in a
gingham dress.

"Leman Pefley!" she exclaimed as he continued toward
her with a boyish smile. "My lands!"

He took off his cap and held it there.

"And so you finally decided to come see us after all!"

"Yes, ma'am. It was my daddy's idea."

"But not yours?"

"Anyway, we brought some presents."

"Ah. But Christmas is over, isn't it?"

"Yes, ma'am. But we needed to pick up my grandmother's presents."

She laughed. She had put in place a certain amount of
bridgework on her teeth. Lee judged her as between 30
and 70 years into her age, a typical representative of his
parents' generation.

"We're going fishing, Dana and me."

"So I heard! You be careful now, you hear?"

Already she was getting bored with him. She appeared
to have seen someone of her own age moving toward her.
"You be careful now."

Again, Lee agreed to do so. Dana was gone; his brother,
too, and in their place a farm boy had come to town riding
on a mule.

By 2:30, Lee had finished with his visitations and was
trundling homeward, tired but happy, when one of the
local youths suddenly stepped out in front of him and
submitted a question. "Now just where in hell do you
think *you're* going?"

Immediately Lee went into a tough facial expression
that expressed everything one needed to know about his
underlying character. "What's it to you?"

"What'd you say? No, I want to know what you said
just now."

"Home. If it's any of your beeswax." He tried to get past, but was unable to do so owing to the second and third boys standing on both sides of the first. And where now, pray, was Cecil when he most was needed? Riding with Margaret, Lee expected, in an old Ford car.

"Anyway, what's that shit you got there in your pocket?"

Lee showed it, a licorice stick given him by one of the downtown clerks. "Aw, it's just a . . . She gave it to me."

"He don't even know what it is!" the third boy said.

"Where're you from? And don't tell me you're from here, 'cause I know you ain't."

Lee pointed to his corner of the state, a far region known for its geologic formations. He was ready to hand over his licorice stick, if that would get him home again. And in any case, given his small size, he had always considered courtesy the better part of recklessness. But mostly it was the second boy who worried him, an older sort of person of some twelve or thirteen years, if Lee wasn't mistaken.

"Besides, you and Dana ain't going to catch nothing tonight. Waste of time."

"We might."

"Naw, shit, you might get an ell or *catfish*, a real small one, but that's about it."

"You're probably right," said Lee, going into a different tack.

"Well, hell yeah, we're right! Besides, you don't have any business down here, anyway."

"I know it. I never wanted to come in the first place. Shoot, you probably won't ever see me again. Not really."

"Well, all right. That's a *whole lot* better, what you just said."

They shook. Already, the first and third boys were getting bored with him, whileas for the second, he had gone off and left them several moments earlier.

The levee was steep, and by the time he had climbed to the top, lo, he could see approximately the whole distance to his own hometown. He saw a field with cattle in it, and beyond that, bright blue segments of the river that wormed its way in and out of the pine forest that entailed the town. He thought again of all those beautiful old women and girls we know nothing of anymore. Such a great deal of history had taken part here, a story also of reptiles, rotifers, and brachiopods dating back to when warm seas had covered much of Alabama itself.

But primarily it were the negro cabins that enchanted the boy, slave dwellings at one time now leaning up against one another for support. He saw a man sleeping on one of the porches, never mind that the weather was too chilly for that. Saw smoke rising from the chimneys, a broken wagon, a yard pot and grindstone lying in the yard. Surveying everything, he detected a child and two hens skulking in the field. Someone had owned a fine new automobile at one period that today was but a burned-out shell lying on its head. He heard gospel music from somewhere, hogs grunting, an airplane moving overhead.

He was being followed by a ramshackle dog with a foot-long tongue. Getting down on one knee, Slade smoothed him down and tried, vainlessly, to look into the creature's eyes which, however, he kept averted at all times. The dog had some history behind him, judging from the damage to his left paw and the abbreviations to his ears and residual tail. What things had he not seen, what midnight adventures, what meals? Two minutes having gone past in this manner, the animal relented finally and permitted Lee to look into his eyes.

He had intended, Sloan, to circumambulate the entire village, an idea that came to nothing when he happened upon that break in the levee where, on a certain bad day in 1928, the rising river had pushed everything aside and come rushing into town. He could still hear the screams, it seemed to him, of negroes and children drowning in the tide, the courthouse flooded up to its elbows in the stuff, the ruined letters with missing ink, destroyed photographs, precious stamps, bills of lading, cash money disgorged from bank vaults, etc., etc. And his own family, too, his grandparents floating up to the ceiling in flooded rooms—he remembered all of it. Inspired by this, he tried to dredge up recollections of an even earlier time, when once again the levee had failed to ward off yet another flood pouring down upon them from out of the stinking North.

The land was doomed, and everywhere he looked, *change* was going forward, the first cause of human unhappiness on Earth. Dialing into the future, he envisioned this whole vista full of a giant city staffed with low-grade individuals, a noisy people striding back and forth to no good purpose. No dogs, no crickets, no midnight fishing with moonlight peeping through the pines. Is that what they wanted?

Yes, and by the time he had returned to the house, his grandmother had prepared an urn of homemade ice cream for him alone. Both boys, his brother included, consumed a great part of it, and then drifted off to widely-separated stations to get some rest. Himself, he preferred the bed in which his grandfather had died. It was an interesting piece of furniture—long and narrow and, like the man himself, so high off the floor that he must use a little staircase to arrive at the surface. Further, the bed had a quilt embroidered with a bible story having to do with Lot's wife and her transformation into salt. The linens smelt of kerosene, mildew, pine oil, and other good things. The curtain was almost transparent, and he could fix upon the Sun deteriorating hurriedly as day wore on.

He loved to come awake at night when most people were tired, but he was at his best. The adult people had meantime gathered in the adjoining room, where Lee could hear them speaking sadly about relationships and business affairs. Life was difficult, and things were hard, and a person had to earn a living in the world. They were also playing dominoes, as Lee could gather from the sound of the quoits. Save for his grandmother, who needed a full minute or more, they played at high speed.

"Dern!" his uncle said. "Pretty much leaves me sucking the hind teat!"

There were other sounds, including the noise of ice cubes clashing in goblets of sweet tea. And then, finally, the smaller sound of his uncle whittling at his nails with the sharpest knife in Alabama. The man went on speaking: "Maybe if he was living down here with us instead of up there with y'all, maybe he wouldn't get into so much trouble all the time."

Lee now came fully awake. It was perhaps seven o'clock in the evening, time to go fishing; instead, the people in the next room were talking about employment, relocation, and about himself. He heard words relating to the town of Enterprise, a sizeable place where the economy was good and new industry was coming to town. But Lee had heard these stories before and knew his father was not likely ever to leave his good position, never mind that it might bring him back to William's House.

Climbing down from his roost, Lee padded to the door and applied his ear to the opening. He could hear ice cubes, his uncle mixing up the dominoes, and the smaller sound of his grandmother jotting down the score—she never lost—on the little yellow pad—they let her win—kept for that purpose. That was when Leland heard his brother speak out loud and clear: "Yeah. If he was down here with y'all, then maybe we could have some peace up *there.*"

"Ought to be 'shamed!" Molly said. "Talkin' that way." She was a great black woman, Molly, of two hundred fifty pounds, who in theory was looking after Leland's grandmother but who in fact came and went at pleasure. And was she, too, playing dominoes? Based upon the woman's mathematical skills, Lee doubted it. He heard then, Lee, a voice that was not familiar to him: "Or, you could send him to one of those military schools."

That did it. Emerging from his chamber, Lee put on a groggy face and began rubbing his eyes as if he had just now come awake. The sixth person in the room had always been a relative of his uncle's wife, as Lee now recollected. His brother, two-thirds asleep, was sitting in their father's lap while assisting with the game. But Lee had been wrong about the tea; in fact, the adults were consuming alcoholic spirits of some nature, all save his grandmother, who had opted for straight buttermilk.

"Shoot!" his uncle said. "We figured you was dead."

"Not yet," Lee said, looking about sadly.

"Should be," his brother contributed.

"Can't have Christmas without you."

"We could if we wanted to."

Lee glanced to the corner of the room and the rather fatigued tree, where a few presents sat at random among the branches. Christmas was several days past; however, his grandmother's calendar was nearly always out of tune. And although he had fingered these gifts the night before without being able precisely to identify the contents, he was only faintly interested in anything his grandmother might have chosen. He would be expected to put on a delighted face all the same.

He sat off to one side, reflecting a greater and greater degree of boredom as the adults continued with the dominoes. It was a genteel game, and they were genteel, too. Seen from behind, he could detect in the tilt of his father's head that the man was having fun. And why not? He was in William's House, and that was his own very mother sitting just across from him. Outside, a few post-season crickets were still stridulating bravely from their posts in

the garden and lawn and, in one or two instances, in the
fretwork that decorated the leeward side of the house.
Suddenly, his father smote himself ruefully on the forehead, as if he had not forfeited the game on purpose.

"Well," said Lee, standing and stretching. "I reckon it's
time to open the presents now."

No one gave attention to him. And was he, really, part
of this family?

"Or maybe we should go fishing first," he said, "and
then open the presents."

No one noticed what he said. His grandmother was tal-
lying the score, while the woman Molly was in the corner
eating ice cream with a large iron fork. As to this latter
person's contribution to his grandmother's safety and
happiness . . . There was none.

"Or, we could . . ."

"Lee?"

"Sir?"

"I reckon you better fetch some more of that good ice
cream for Molly over there."

And so that was it, that at age eleven he had come to
waiting on negresses. He arose, kicked at the rug, made a
couple of faces, and was actually about to trudge off toward the icebox when his uncle said this: "We'll go fishing
in a little bit."

"Yes, sir. But I'm thinking we ought to open the presents first."

"Are?"

"Yeah."

The adults all looked up at him.

"Yes, *sir*, I mean."

There were but three gifts, sloppy-looking affairs
wrapped in birthday paper. It was Lee's hope and expectation that, once he had seen what was inside them, he'd
be better able to focus upon the evening's major event.

Accordingly, he went to the tree and brought back a small, square box addressed to Molly. (There were no presents for the adults, none.) She had been given, Molly, two pale handkerchiefs, very delicate, with her initials on them, together with a tiny but highly articulated jar of French perfume. She lauded these and held the amber-colored fragrance to the light. In color, it resembled the spirituous liquor they had been drinking all night.

It has been said that his father received nothing; truth was, his grandmother has passed a five-dollar bill to Leland's father earlier that day, an enormous sum according to her memory. It was to fit just about perfectly into the leathern billfold given him by Lee. And in truth Lee could not think of anything adults appreciated more.

His own present was far the heaviest and consisted, once he had opened it, of a really first-class gift. Lee grinned widely. "Good Lord!"

"We didn't get things like that when I was a kid. Just hope you appreciate it."

"I think he does. Look at that grin."

"Gollee!" said Lee. "Thanks a lot!"

Came now the time for his parents' gift to Leland's grandmother, an expensive appliance that by the time of Lee's next visit had been relegated to the barn.

"Good gracious alive." (Dana.) "Looks like one of those electric things they're always talking about."

"And a great big old can of coffee to go with it, too. Shoot."

He ran downstairs, Leland, and after mustering his fishing equipment, hastened over to Dana's where, to his chagrin, his brother had gotten there before him. The house was as fresh and neat as a five-dollar bill and boasted a small collection of bird eggs in a glassed-in case. But Lee's eye was more especially for the rifle that hung over the fireplace, an heirloom that had cost the lives of a pretty good number of Pennsylvania men. Lee gloated over it and hungered for it, and for its sake would have traded away his stamp collection. The man also owned an appreciable collection of government pamphlets and agricultural books, not to mention the stand-up photograph of his two sons then serving in the Atlantic Theater. Lee came closer, recognizing in the younger of those sons the courage and good looks, the indignation, pertinacity, and high intelligence that had always figured so conspicuously in the family. He took up one of the pamphlets and opened it to a woodcut engraving scene of someone gutting a hog.

Dana's car, it turned out, had no radio, and there was a hole in the floor. Indeed, the vehicle was past its better years and could in no wise be compared to that of Leland's father. Nor his profession, nor could that be measured against an engineer. He was, however, the root and nub of the family, and his decisions generally given the first consideration by everybody. Entering the car in his lordly fashion, Lee was disturbed to see that his brother had arrived there already and taken the front seat. A congealed paint brush lay on the floor, along with a crumpled-up cigarette package, a few undelivered letters, and other debris.

"I'm going to catch a fish so big . . ." Lee's brother was saying. He was dressed in a jacket, and the bill of his cap was so far too long that his profile looked more like a duck's than like his own. ". . . so big."

"Well, I hope you do."

It was a serious time, the three of them squinting forward silently into the black, dark night. Lee espied a raccoon caught in the beams, an irrational one who already had crossed the road but who now turned suddenly and ran back whence he had come. The woods were dark and thick, rather like a wall than like anything actually permeable by a human being. The Moon, too, was three-fourths full, and had a counteractive effect on what otherwise had been a chilly night.

Dana's negro lived in a hill-top shack that overlooked the river itself. Here, too, Lee saw the requisite items—a grindstone on the porch, a yard pot and dog, and a wash-tub full of unshelled corn.

"It's me, Blue. So you don't need to shoot us."

They went in. It was a standard shack of the Alabama kind, a two-room affair with a mattress on the floor, a stack of firewood (poorly arranged), and a bucket in place of a commode. The home did have good flooring, but no crown moldings anywhere. Apparently, the man had been eating out of a can of beans, but had lost interest halfway through the project. But what was most characteristic of him was his paucity of legs, both of them having been hewn away many years ago in a famous mishap having to do with one of the downriver sawmills. The owner not only paid him for that day but let him suggest his replacement. There was no light in that cabin save what came from a bed of coals pulsing in the fireplace.

"Ready to go fishing, Blue?"

"Yas, sir, 'spect so."

He had been surprised already that night, Leman, but what followed now surprised him even more—his uncle lifting the man in both arms and carrying him to the car. True, he could not have weighed very much, old as he was and with so much of his previous person buried in the cold, hard ground. Lee followed behind in the wake of the continuing comments that issued from the negro.

"Yas, sir! Awright!"

"We're going to catch us some *fish* tonight, Blue. Leland's brother here, he's going to catch the biggest one."

"'Spec so, yas, sir. Hee, hee."

The drive was short, and by the time they came to the river, the negro had dropped off to sleep. They stood about, Leland's brother and Lee, as Dana again gathered up the man and stowed him into the boat and propped him up. It was not a large vessel, and the dog had to move back and forth between the bow and transom several times before finding a dry place in which to settle

They pushed off. The river was swift and tended to swirl the boat in a circle before finally choosing its direction. Lee put on a bored face, a stratagem that sometimes served to calm his nerves. His brother meantime had taken up in the foremost position and, with the bill of his cap pointing out the route, was trembling visibly.

"They're right down . . . *there*," he explained, pointing into the depths where the great ones slept.

"Yas, sir! 'Spect so."

"You're liable to fall in, too, if you ain't careful."

They passed under the branches of a cottonwood, the foliage offering temporary protection against the blasts of moonlight that made the surface of the river like a silver photograph. Down below, colored lanterns glowed in the chambers of Silurian houses. Could aught be more strange than this, a substance too tenuous to support almost anything? That was why the bottom was as it was, which is to say layered in a rich, green precipitate called *ooze*. Yes, and he could remember his laughter when first he had heard that word.

"Try one of these here *catawba* worms," his uncle said, offering the container.

(And had the man spent his whole afternoon collecting these things?)

"Cast over yonder. You might catch something."

Lee cast. It *was* a good area, judging by the ripples that hinted at activities going on below. Lee concentrated, using his Will upon those three or four cubic feet of water. They had to *eat*, those creatures, and so why not eat worms? Next, he shut his eyes so as better to experience even the subtlest nibbles. Far away he heard an owl blaring and something running barefooted through the woods. Further downstream, he saw what looked like tiny islands or abandoned automobiles bobbing out to sea.

That was when Dana brought in his first fish, one of your ordinary crappies weighing about a pound. Many times had he heard, Leland, how good his uncle was at this particular sport.

"Gollee. You must be the best fisherman in the whole state of . . ."

The man snorted at him, saying, "Shoot. My granddaddy now, he was a whole lot better fisherman than me."

"Well, sure. *Everybody* was better in those days."

They were getting along very well, it seemed to Dana and to Lee. Meantime the man called Blue had brought in a very similar fish that effectively doubled their catch for the day. But apart from the fish, the negro was chagrined to have lost his worm.

"Stolt my wurm!"

"We got more."

"Stolt it!"

The boat was taking them where it wanted, and meantime Leland had caught nothing. That was when he discovered for the first time that some twenty or thirty further negroes were positioned at intervals up and down the shore, all of them with fishing poles and all, save one, maintaining perfect silence. Hard to discern in the pitch-black night, Lee counted four more on the opposite bank. One, an elderly sort of person, had been blinded by the yellow Moon and was wearing colored glasses. Lee waved, getting no response at all. (He knew, of course, that these people were much less courteous at night when they could be identified but by family members only.) Having been pushed to shore by the tide, Blue began conferring in dialect with two young children who offered no danger to the persons in the boat. Lee listened keenly, picking up just "white trash" and not much else.

The night was clear, the river swift, and by morning time they could have drifted all the way to Florida. Lee was ready for that.

"Tired of fishing already?" his uncle asked.

"Aw, I won't catch anything."

"Good gracious alive. I believe you're just like your daddy was."

"We could come back *later*."

"Hm?"

"Later."

"My gracious, I believe you're even *worse* than your daddy was!"

"He is!" Leland's brother said, raising his hand for recognition.

They had come a great distance by now and could look forward to a lot of rowing to get them back home again. The river was clean and vacant, and now that Dana and Blue had each caught two or three further fish, Lee could see no reason for tiring himself even more.

"We could come back tomorrow, for example."

It was just that moment that Leland's brother lurched wildly to one side, having hooked into what undoubtedly would prove the biggest catch of the night. He had been expecting it, Lee had.

"My gracious!" Dana said.

The dog barked.

Lee spoke no more. In all sincerity, he hoped the fish would get away. It was not a good thing, always to be out-classed by a character of that age.

"He's going to get away," said Lee. "I can tell."

"No. No, I don't hardly think so."

They had to use the net. It was, of course, a bass, a three- or four-pound example going through a delirium of joy for being given freedom at last. It was a significant catch, even if in return for it his brother had lost his hat in the water.

They coasted downriver for another quarter-mile or more before Leland opted to bed down in the bottom of the boat. He estimated that it was somewhere between eight and eleven o'clock and that he ought to get some rest before dealing with any further catches. A wind had come up, dislodging some of the minor stars. He heard a train shrieking in the night. Except for time and space, he might himself be on board that train, among the stewards and dining cars and the rest. Time, dread time that turns girls to dust, and light, what on earth was *that*? And *death*, yes indeed, and *time*—which is to say until he remembered that he had already dealt with that one just a few days ago.

Eleven

He woke between clean sheets. He could hear dogs barking, some of them inside the house. And then too, of course, there were those smells of bacon and eggs, of waffles made of buttermilk served with a choice of honey and/or several kinds of jam. He could smell coffee as well, even if he wasn't yet allowed any. Adults were talking, he could hear an airplane overhead, the tolling of the downtown bells, a rooster, a wagon, and his grandmother's hogs harmonizing to the Sun. And in short, it was another golden January morning in the Alabama of that day.

He jumped into his trousers and, after reporting to the bathroom and coming back, got into his shirt as well. So much the greater, then, was his dismay to find the waffles gone, all but one, and his people in their Sunday clothes.

"Maybe I'll stay home today," Lee offered, reaching for the waffle.

They laughed, the whole room. He had as much opportunity of staying home on a Sunday as of being poured a fresh cup of coffee with whiskey in it.

"I saved a waffle for you," his grandmother said helpfully.

Lee thanked her.

"I tried to save another one, too."

She had done as well as she could, given the company.
Suddenly Lee jumped back, astonished at the length of his
father's cigarette ash. Indeed, his lap was full of the stuff.
And was this not the very same chair in which he had sat
as a boy when of about Leland's age? Indubitably. And on
the wall the very same painting of fruits pouring from a
cornucopia, of General Wolfe expiring on the Plains of
Abraham, and, in a much smaller etching not much larger
than a playing card, of a bearded man lost now to family
memory. Comparing himself to that one, Lee could see
the resemblance between them, of good intentions
brought to a close by early death.

This time he chose orange marmalade in place of honey and washed it down with a dense buttermilk full of
curds. (Let him stay here but for a single season and he'd
have grown as healthy as Cecil.) He had hoped and had
expected that his grandmother's negro would prepare a
new bowl of waffle batter, but when after a few minutes
had gone past and the woman refused to meet his stare,
he gave up on it. No coffee, and in the end he was reduced
to a single fried egg with a punctured sac.

How he loathed his Sunday suit! It was a cumbersome
ensemble in five parts, much more constrictive by far than
his ballroom clothes. There was a tie, too, a highly limp
one with someone else's armorial on it, if armorial was
what it was. (Cecil's tie, on the other hand, bore the picture of a girl in a bathing suit.) Even so, he adorned himself in his shirt and tie and coat and vest, and then spent
ten minutes working on himself in the mirror while trying
to ameliorate the effect. He still looked like a queer, however. Very glad was he that Gwen and the others couldn't
see him at this minute.

It was a solid piece of work, the downtown Methodist
church, as were all the structures made by his grandfather.
It gave Lee a somewhat peculiar feeling to know that Poor

Albert had driven some of the nails and, under the super-
vision of his stern father, had mixed the actual concrete.
Moving with solemnity, the family now entered the building, with Lee forming the next-to-last person in line.
Again he jumped back, this time with greater force than
before, upon seeing that his brother had found his fishing
hat and was wearing it in these hallowed precincts. Lee
nodded to the distinguished-looking woman in the second
pew whose own chapeau was even more peculiar-looking
than his brother's. He was aware that people were smiling
down upon them with approval, including even the negroes in the balcony, one more result of his extinct grandfather's reputation among these people. And Lee waved
back, too, which is to say until his father nudged him forward.

The church held three hundred people, and a good
thirty or forty of them were blood connections of his. The
organist, also a family member, was good at his work, and
soon Lee began to be affected by the music, which turned
his mind back in the direction of a restored Confederacy,
except this time we won. Meantime he had descried a
pretty girl in one of the middle pews whom he refused to
look at, however, never knowing whether she might not
also be a connection of his.

He had always admired stained-glass windows, especially those that seemed to exhibit living conditions back
when life was so much more vivid and brilliant than in
these latter days. Day after day and year after year, the
world was growing greyer and greyer, the colors leaching
away even as the economy grew stronger—a philosophy of
his that was to confirm itself as he grew older.

The sermon turned out to be a good one, pretty good,
and had served to refresh his grandmother to a considerable extent. And if her hat were the most peculiar of all,
and though her purse be made of lace, and though it hang
down by a foot or more, and her shoes be black and

square and she carry a jackknife in her pocket, even so she had no continuing worries except for her house and its things, and thoughts of her defunct husband. Lee, along with the rest of the congregation, stood now and waited graciously for his family to file out into the Sun. It was a bright day, good for fishing, for hot biscuits and sweet tea and the half dozen pretty girls in their dresses who had come together on the porch of the church that Leland's grandfather had built. Seldom had he experienced such a sharp desire to go over and join any other such group of people.

"Hi!" he said, striding straight toward them and then, without having to mention its significance, revealing his last name. "But we're leaving in a few hours, actually."

The girls came suddenly together in a huddle and whispered to each other. In the beginning he had singled out the one in the yellow dress, but as he approached nearer and could see more clearly, his choice fell upon a brown-headed girl who seemed somewhat more relaxed than the others and had a knowing smile. It occurred to him that she might be intelligent, a new and strange experience for him. Veering away from her at the last instant, he went back to the girl in yellow. She was still sunburned from last summer, and her hands were gnarly and most likely strong.

"I'm one of Dana's friends."

They nodded and then rushed together again to consult about it. They were shyer than the big-city girls of his acquaintance, and except for the intelligent one, had been waiting for years, as it seemed to him, for someone like him. He knew of no law, no dictates from his parents, to prevent him from having girlfriends in two different towns.

"Shoot," he went on. "If I didn't live in ———" (he provided the name of the town in which he actually lived), "I wouldn't mind living right here!"

Two of them giggled, and two of them blushed. Meantime his taste had rotated over onto the girl in green, a dewy personality about as compliant-looking as any he had ever seen. Focusing upon her alone, he said, "Boy, I thought the girls in ———" (see above) "were pretty! Boy, was I wrong!"

And that, of course, was when his mother—it never failed—began calling for him. And yet Lee, who had more lief to die at once than be seen obeying anyone, went on speaking: "But I'm coming back when school is out."

"Free country."

"And I'll be coming to church, too."

"We always come."

They nodded at each other, especially the green one.

From there the family drove back to the big house again, a half-mile journey that was hard upon Leland's humpbacked grandmother, who didn't really fit into a modern car. And then, too, she hated to be away from William's House for very long lest someone come and take away her love letters, her canned fruits, her quilts and doilies, and things in her closet. Her head, such as it was, was small and football-shaped, and yet he was as convinced that she had some experiences stored away in there as that she had no intention of discussing them with anyone. Lee came nearer, catching a whiff of her nineteenth-century perfume. She had been the prettiest girl in the world at one time, and even, some said, one of the prettiest in the county.

Her possessions were intact, and by the time Lee had changed out of his humiliating costume and into usable clothes, it was time for ice cream and cantaloupe. He watched with fascination as his uncle opened his knife, and after slicing the melon into pieces, picked them up one by one on the tip of his blade. It was only just one o'clock in the afternoon with hours still to go before it

were dark again and time for dominoes. Suddenly, feeling
that he might be in danger of getting bored, Lee arose and
excused himself, and went out to the barn.

One thin beam of sunlight fell through the roof and set
up a spot on the floor, Lee's favorite place in which to sit.
Twenty years had gone by since last the building had been
put to practical use, and Lee was conscious, as it were, of
having been summoned to life in the *aftermath* of history,
leaving him with very little that still needed to be done.
These dead cows and mules, his disappeared grandfathers,
they had done the essential work, carrying it out with rude
tools that Lee could barely name. His sympathy went out
even to the crickets and bees, whole generations of them
condemned to lifelong missions of great tediousness. It
also went out for his grandmother, still treadling away (insofar as she was able) on her sewing machine. And therefore, although his own life might turn out to be interesting
and good, it was too late to atone for all the hard work
that had gone on before him—such was his philosophy
then *and* later.

Twelve

They drove in silence back to Lee's hometown. The day
was crystalline, a few generalized clouds limping past
overhead in skies of purple-brown. Lee's father, on the
other hand, was noticeably less cheerful than of just a
couple of hours ago. He did so hate it, abandoning his an-
cestral house to the vagaries of time and cold weather. Lee
kept silent therefore and sat looking straight ahead. The
roadside signs were numerous enough, but offered much
too little reading matter to keep him occupied. They
passed a tin-roof shack, out front a man laboring in his
garden on a Sunday. Yes, one could do worse than to ride
in bright sun through a series of nonreplicable moments
in history and time. And because for him life was but a

hoard of old and fading photographs conserved in the album of the mind.

They passed a man hiking down the highway with one foot lifted forever in midair. Came next his own hometown, a silvery portrait in which some of last week's Christmas decorations had been left in place. His headache today, Lee's, was a routine affair, almost negligible indeed, and he was in the grip of an emotional serenity redolent of optimism. They passed Lee's favorite domestic building, a two-story pile, well-glazed, with blue shutters and a mob of plastic flamingoes in the yard. He caught a quick view of Chichi Roberts whistling homeward from the library with three or four books under his arm and then, next, old man Dooley striding down Seventh Street with a cigar in his mouth and a dog on his leash. He would remember this, Leland would, and in that way distinguish himself as the only person in history to have done so.

Arriving home, Lee helped to unload the car and then rushed to the upstairs mirror to find whether he still existed or not. He could see himself in two dimensions and then, with his finger, could verify the third. Could anything be more hideous than this? To see one's self and know that it was looking back? Delaying there, he went through several facial expressions ranging from tragedy to gladness and back. (As long as he lived, he was never to decide whether he lacked something, or whether it was the other way around.) And that, of course, was when his brother yelled out loud and clear: "He's doing it again!"

Conditions improved during the remainder of the day, and by late afternoon he could have been found lying in the parlor among the funny pages. He had wanted to keep abreast of the actions of Foozy and Alley Oop, and took care to set off to one side the sheet with *Mutt and Jeff,* lest his father come looking for it in an irritable state. These personalities added to the town's population, and he knew at least as much about them as about the man next door. For example, he saw himself as a good deal like Foozy, while his brother appeared to have been modeled on Perry Winkle. Comforted by that, he fell asleep at 4:45 in the afternoon on January 6.

He awoke to the sound of the radio confiding in his ear. Could anything be more strange than that—radio? For all he knew, the man doing the speaking had died several minutes ago, before his voice had been loaded aboard the wire. Lee still hoped to adjust himself to these inventions and take his place in the modernity coming up all around them. Familiar by now with radios and cars, he had already disposed of his pencils, most of them, and taken up with ball-point pens.

Thirteen

Thus Lee, who now returned to his usual ways. The route to school was still the same, though it disturbed him to find that instead of parking his car with the nose pointing eastward, today Old Man Dooley had done it in the opposite direction. Confused by that, the boy grew pensive at first, and then morose. Yes, and someday huge glaciers of ice would cover the town and all the girls he knew would have come and gone and have consummated their fates at last.

It was the essential nature of things that bothered Lee—of gawky human beings walking upright on the soles of hairless feet while striving to communicate, each to each, with uvulas and mouth parts. Shoes they wore, and while dressed in woolen stuffs, gazed about surreptitiously with jellied eyes that, nauseatingly, were outgrowths of the brain itself. Rodents were lovelier than this.

"Something wrong with you," said Leland to himself.

"I know, I know. But I don't care."

Arriving earlier than usual, he wandered about in the schoolyard, trying to reacquaint himself with the cast of people he had known. It relieved him to see that Naomi, the girl who liked him, was otherwise occupied. Meantime the beautiful Barbara Milkens was standing off by herself, while not very far away Cecil appeared to be locked in conversation with someone's older sister. Lee went to him and waited.

"I thought we was rid of you," the boy said.

Lee grinned.

"Lee, meet Sandra. Sandra, this here is Sloan."

They shook. Seen at this range, the girl was somewhat prettier than he had reckoned. She had two moles, wee ones, that looked like dots of ink on the aft side of her heart-shaped lips. It dawned on him that Cecil had exchanged his other girl for this one.

"Hey, I thought you were going with Barbara!"

"I was. But now *we're* going together, her and me."

"How come!"

"It's personal. Shut up."

"Yeah, but . . . !"

"Thought I told you to shut up."

"Okay. But I want to get *her* side of the story."

He turned and walked to where Barbara was waiting. She did not appear to be unhappy, in spite of matters.

"Hi," he said. "Say, I thought you were going with Cecil. You used to."

"Oh, Cecil! He makes me want to vomit! I think he should just get married and settle down!"

"He's too young."

"He is *not* too young! Believe me."

"Good Lord. Well, who are you going with now?" (He was giving her the sort of concentrated attention that, according to his sources, women crave. She was dressed in a purple sweater that had enough room in it for the figure that would soon be hers.)

"Nobody. And I'm not going to for a *long, long* time."

"I don't blame you! How long?"

She turned and looked him in the face. Below the surface she seemed to be smiling faintly with some of her smaller facial muscles. "Maybe *we* can go together someday, Lee. If you promise to be nice."

"Okay, when?"

"When you're fourteen."

"Be dead by then."

She laughed out loud at him, a good indication he believed.

The professoress was older than she should have been and had aged during the three days he had been away. On her desk still rested two gifts that either she hadn't seen or feared to unwrap. Where was Smitty? Lee barely recognized him in his formal shirt. A note came past, a two-page composition in yellow ink. Far away Lee could hear traffic in the road, a dog barking from the hills, an individual tiptoeing down the hall, toilets flushing, and the more distant sound of screams from the Principal's office. Those who scream deserve it, in Leland's opinion.

He had full intended to join the rest of his class in the cafeteria; instead, Cecil came up from behind and seized him by the throat.

"What, you want to be with us or with them?"

"Us."

"Well all right!"

They went to the Canteen. Lee, his eyes all times open for the high school girl who had forced a kiss on him back in October, ordered a cheeseburger and Orange Drink, and so did Cecil. The last he wanted, Lee, was for the Navy veteran to come and sit with them and light up a cigarette, all of which of course he did. Again, Lee would have preferred to sit quietly and listen to some of the new music, including especially Billy Eckstine's "Prisoner of Love," a song that described almost perfectly his own present predicament. And then, too, seldom had the place been as dark as today it was or contain as many high school girls. In the green room, he caught sight of a blonde girl dancing in a way that made him indignant at first, but less so as time went on. Where was Cecil? The year was 1951 and the scholars were again discussing that knife fight of last month. That was when the veteran turned and looked him in the face, disappointed apparently to be sitting next to an eleven-year-old who didn't smoke, didn't drink, and had no tattoos anywhere.

"Here," he said, forcing a cigarette onto the boy. "Smoke it."

"Naw."

"Goddamn it!"

"Okay, I will."

Sooner or later, it was something that had to be done. He speculated that it might actually be a pleasure of some kind; instead, it proved just about as bad as anything in his experience. Nor did he understand how properly to hold the thing in the received way. Another of his favorite songs, "Stranger on the Shore," had come on, and he had wanted to remain clear-headed for it. Cecil meantime had gone off into the green room where from time to time Lee was able to identify his silhouette moving about in the dark. All might still have been well had not the high school girl just then spotted him among the tables. Lee tried but failed to get out of her line of vision. And the next he knew, she had arisen from her place and was proceeding toward him.

"Hi," Lee said.

"Been hiding from me!"

"No, ma'am!"

"Hiding!"

"I been out of town."

"Yes, hiding," she said for the third time. "You're so bad."

He allowed her to pry loose the cigarette and then bring it up to her own lips and draw on it. He could also see that three or four other high school people were watching with amusement from the bar.

"So bad. I guess I'm just going to have to . . ."

She did it—moving to one side and climbing into his lap. Her weight was greater than his, but not so much greater that he elected to push her away. She was deliberately wearing makeup on her face, including red lipstick. Lee, his kneecaps trembling, looked off into the distance and put on a thoughtful expression. He had lost his cigarette and meantime, where was Cecil? He had no decent way to fend off the kiss that now began to close in upon him, a prolonged business in which he knew for a certainty that he was getting lipstick on him.

"You're so bad," she said, whispering confidentially into his ear. These words affected him, creating a kind of numbness in certain parts. He now began to realize that his very favorite all-time song had just now come on, a gift from providence that not in a thousand years would be repeated.

Beware, my foolish heart,
her lips are much too close to mine.

He had been smoking and drinking, and now he was kissing in full view of fifteen or twenty high school people hooting at him. His fame was increasing, no question about that. It needn't have come as any great surprise, therefore, when the school's chief disciplinarian suddenly came into the place and saw what he was doing. All Lee had ever wanted was a few moments of privacy; instead, he found himself once more in the outside world, once more being prodded at speed over to the Principal's office.

Reversal of fortune? He was getting used to it. Seating himself in his accustomed place, he strove to make conversation with a frightened-looking seventh-grader who had never visited this place before.

"Don't worry," Leland said. "You get used to it after a while."

"Does it hurt?"

"Hurt? He'll make you wish you'd never been born!"

"Oh, God. It's just not fair!'

"That ain't got nothing to do with it. Anyway, I'm going to die anyway. So what difference does it make?"

"Oh yeah, I heard about that. Because of your gizzard, you mean?"

"Right."

Just now, the Principal was working on one of the football players, a largish individual showing more weakness than Lee would have expected of him.

"That makes seven," Lee said. "Licks."

"Oh, God."

"We'll just have to wait and see whether he gets ten or maybe twenty. Smitty got a hundred last year."

"Twenty!"

"*I* got twenty-five. About a month ago."

"Dang! Maybe that's what did it to your gizzard."

"Probably." He was close to tears. It appalled him that the stenographer, an older woman with a reticulated face, seemed entirely unconcerned with what was transpiring in the other room. Her job had hardened her to all such considerations—this was Lee's theory about the matter. Looking directly at her, he was about to say something when the door came open and the football player rushed from the room.

"Next!"

Lee stood. He had been given no time to get into the extra sets of underwear stored away in his desk for the purpose, no, nor time to prepare himself mentally or bring his Will into play. Even so, he entered the chamber with a bored expression and seated himself on the leathern couch that looked out over the floor-to-ceiling bookcase with its untidy arrangement.

"Hi," he said.

The man had aged. Slowly, he lifted his head and gazed at Lee as if he had never seen this person before. It was tenebrous in there, and except for the man's sparkling glasses, Lee would not have been able to pinpoint him in the gloom.

"Leward, is it?"

"Yes, sir."

"Reading anything these days?"

Lee recited the list of the two books he had been given as Christmas presents, literary stuff, one of them, and the other pure fluff. Having finished, he observed that the man once again had put his head down on the desk.

"Killing Germans when we should have been doing it to Russians."

"Sir?"

"Oh yes, and now we've got us a *new* war going on over there. Could have won it, too, if they hadn't fired MacArthur."

"I read *The Swiss Family Robinson*."

"Yes, and I expect you could recite it by now. Lee, Lee, Lee. Are you ready?"

He rose, Lee, and took up his position in the center of the room. He feared for his tailbone, but except for that he expected the man to give him only a few unimportant blows before tiring of it. So much, therefore, was the greater of his surprise when the man delivered no blows at all.

"It just gets worse and worse with you, Leward. Canteen again—is that what it was? Except this time, you got Sophie in your lap and a bunch of cigarettes in your mouth."

"You going to whip her, too?" the boy dared to ask.

"Hm? No, that's high school stuff. Some of those gentlemen could whip *me*. Ready to take your punishment?"

Lee raised his hand to answer, but the man never called on him. Instead, he strode quickly to his cabinet and took out his *haruspication* hat, he called it.

"Lee, Lee, Lee. I see a people that cares less about their own babies and wives than about playing poker and drinking gin. You going to be like that when you grow up?"

"Not the cigarettes."

"A world of starving babies?"

"They won't do that."

"But they will! I'm the one wearing the hat."

Far away and over the hill and back, he thought that he could hear music coming from the Canteen, where people were dancing.

"Anyway, I'll be dead by then."

"Might be glad you are." And then: "Lee, Lee, Lee; I can foresee the day when women will be like men and outright negroes will sleep in the best hotels. Don't laugh."

Never laughing, Lee abandoned his awkward position, went back to the chair, and seated himself. The day was long and Time was, too, and he had still two full classes before he could go home and cozy up next to the radio and sleep away the remains of the afternoon.

Wrong about the radio and wrong about home, he found Naomi waiting for him by the gate. He was flattered, he supposed, but had tried so hard to keep out of view during the past few days that he was shocked to be reminded of her actual presentation. In mathematical terms, she was perhaps twenty percent as beautiful as Barbara and about thirty-five of Gwen. On the other hand, she was a good one hundred fifty percent of certain others he could have named. He was thinking about this, march-

ing straight forward with the girl at his side, when he espied his own appearance in the dime-store window.

"Want to go to the post office?" he respectfully inquired.

They turned in that direction. The building was open
at all hours and had the finest collection of wanted posters
anywhere. Just then, Preston breezed past on his bicycle,
almost coming to a stop when he remarked these two in
company with one another. And now the town knew, too.
The movie theater was open already, but Lee had no need
for this particular feature. Cary Grant? Not when for the
same money he could have seen The Bowery Boys' most
recent film.

They moved past the old Roman wall where for the
past years a team of archeologists had been digging. They
passed the tobacco shop, inside it one or two old men trying to read some of the material without paying for it. And
then, finally, just before they arrived at the post office, a
grocery store with a lonely-looking man in an apron
among his fruits and vegetables.

It was unnerving in those days to enter this building
owing to the three grim men, triplets perhaps, who sat
looking out from behind their bespoken grilles. A person
could buy a stamp in this place, or receive a package, or
take advantage of the restroom, but what he could *not* do
was discover any inflection whatsoever in any of those
faces.

"Hi," Lee said.

The posters themselves hung from a hook on the wall.
Standing on tiptoes, Lee rifled hurriedly through the first
three or four of them until he came to a person of such
empty eyes and abysmal-looking character that he knew
very well he would be dreaming about him tonight.

"Look at that one," he whispered to the girl next to
him.

"Gosh. What did *he* do?"

"Mail fraud," Lee answered somewhat disappointedly. "But he probably did lots of other things, too."

"My uncle, he . . ."

Lee cut her off. Amazingly, the next poster featured an individual even worse than the prior one.

"Dang! Shoot, he'll cut your throat for you so fast you won't even have time to think about it."

They lingered over the photograph for a considerable time. The man was evil, but yet willing to carry out actions that most people wouldn't have dared even in causes that were good—this was Lee's thinking at that particular time. He noted then that Steven, his friend from school, had entered the place with pad and pencil and had begun taking information from the posters.

"Hi," Lee said.

The next picture was of a woman—Lee jumped back— a woman who among other behaviors was most certainly a whore, whether they mentioned that or not.

"Poor thing."

"Poor thing! Look at her!"

"Maybe she can't help it."

The next individual was a negro, and the one after that had no photograph at all, so successful had he been. Reading the text, Lee discovered that he had committed crimes both in North and South America, and likely other places as well.

"What did *he* do?" the girl asked.

"I don't know. Something about stocks and bonds."

That was when the middle postman, the one whose facial expression was the most unchangeable, said, "Okay, I reckon you people have been hanging around here long enough."

It was the first time Lee had heard him speak. He was about to comply, Lee, when his girlfriend spoke up loud and clear: "We have just as much right as you do!"

"No, you don't."

Steven had disappeared.

"You get on out of here, or I'll put the police on you. I mean it."

"Anyway, we were just fixing to leave anyway."

"Good."

The day had clouded in their absence, but not so much that the weather was not still bright and chill, a few fast-running clouds hastening past overhead. This unimportant moment for no good reason subsumed itself into Leland's mind, there to fester for the next five hundred years.

"It's not fair! We have just as much right as he does!"

"I know it. Hey, you want to go over there?"

It was, of course, the pawnshop, Leland's third-favorite location in the entire city.

"If you want to," said she, after they had arrived there.

"Look at all those things!"

His eye was for the knives, devilish objects, some of them with scenes and mottoes inscribed on the blade. *Her* eye, by contrast, was for a small, white puppy who had been set up in the adjoining window with a ribbon about its neck. The next he knew, she had gotten down on one knee and was striving to converse with the animal. This had the effect of showing off her shoes, oversize objects that, apparently, had come down to her from her brothers and/or father. He was in this situation, Lee, that she was what she was, and yet he was in love with her, presumably. That was when his vision ran up against a pile of coins that glinted in the Sun, some of them with particular inscriptions. Pressing at the glass, he was able to make out the graven portraits and brief texts that described their value. The girl meantime had arisen and was gazing in at a tray of jewels and earrings and the like. It occurred to Lee that their tastes ran naturally to very unlike objects. She had fixed upon a brooch that Lee would have said was perfect junk, had anyone asked.

There were guitars and other instruments, also a gaunt proprietor trying to signal them inside. Suddenly (he jumped back) his eye ricocheted off a pudgy stamp album left open at New Caledonia. A thousand years might go by, and still he'd not have as many stamps as that. It pained him, especially a certain imperforate with the portrait of an ostrich on it.

"Look at this one," he called.

She came, looked, looked at him, and went away again. It was almost four o'clock in the afternoon and he had to make haste if he hoped to get to the drugstore before too late.

It smelled of ice cream in there, not to mention cheeseburgers and Orange Drinks. Putting on a bored face, Lee bellied up to the counter and began reading through the menu with an air of disappointment.

"How much," he asked, "are these nutritious, delightfully fresh banana splits with three different kinds of ice cream?"

She cited the price, the woman behind the counter, doing it in a style even more impatient than Lee's.

"Well, how about one of these yummy vanilla ice cream sodas?" he asked.

"Just like it says. Fifteen cents."

"What do you want?" he asked the girl.

"Nothing. You got lipstick on your shirt."

"Okay, how about an Orange Drink?"

She nodded enthusiastically. For all he knew, she, too, might have money in case he ran dry. Having submitted his order, he again searched the menu, but came up with nothing further that lay inside his budget. Watching the girl, he determined that she might actually end up as the prettiest girl in school. But he doubted it. A man in a hat had entered the place, but whether he had come for contraceptives or medicine or to flirt with the clerk, Lee could not right away declare. He had missed the two best radio shows of the day, but was confident that Carl would bring him up to date later on.

"Well," he said, once they had vacated the place. "Guess I better get on home."

"Me, too. We're having meatloaf tonight."

"And I got lots of homework, too. Which is not even to mention Smitty's."

"And sweet tea."

"I don't know *what* we're having. Liver, probably."

They laughed, both. They were getting along very well, it seemed to Lee, and appeared to share a number of things. They shook then, and parted, she to her place and he his.

Ended thus Leland's first recorded date.

Fourteen

And so on Wednesday next, while breakfasting on toast and jelly, he learned that he was being withdrawn from school and sent to school in another city. Lee was stunned. Was it purely on account of his smutty behavior or had his father, as they claimed, actually contracted some sort of business arrangement down there?

It was a poor sort of day with rain threatening, a tepid Sun, and his brother following warily at a distance of about two hundred yards. He waited only briefly for Cherise to come along, and when she failed to do so, he took a detour between two of the homes and came out at the intersection of Twelfth and Quintard. No longer did he carry whole books with him on his trek to school; on the contrary, he had learned to snip out the relevant pages and carry these alone. It was an easier thing, and the weight was lighter, too. He also preferred to slip those pages into his vest pocket, a tactic that increased his mobility and left both hands free for self-defense. Now, putting on an astute expression, he took up with his long-time habit of memorizing the town and its people against the time when he would no longer live there.

The schoolyard was full of people organized in little groups. By hap, Lee found himself standing just next to Cecil, wearing a new black leather jacket never seen before. Where *did* that boy get his money? Leland asked himself. By working for it, he replied. Moving around to Cecil's other side, he was able to stay out of Naomi's view.

"Looks like it's going to rain," Lee said. "Anyway, we're moving."

"Get out."

"No, we really are. Moving to ———." He gave the name of the little country town that possessed neither any movie theater nor ballroom classes, nor people like Cecil or Sandra or even himself.

"You ain't going nowhere."

"Got no choice."

"And how about Naomi? You just going to run off and leave her, is that what it is? And who's going to do my math for me?"

"I could come visit her."

"Yeah. But you won't."

"And Steve is a lot better at math than me."

"He dudn't share with people. It's just the way he is."

Lee looked down. Steve was good at health and civics, less so with long division.

"I'm getting real mad at you Slade. Just thought you might want to know."

"Yeah, but . . . !"

"We're all mad, *all* of us." (He indicated around at the schoolyard, a gesture that included several of Leland's enemies as well.) "No, I think you need to reconsider, that's my advice."

"Okay, I will," quoth Lee hurriedly. Gwendolyn was standing close by amid a circle of girls; going to her, Lee took off his cap and addressed the group: "Well, looks like we're leaving, my family and me."

"Oh, gosh. I hope you're just kidding again."

"No! No, we're leaving alright. No question about it."

She seemed somewhat saddened. The others seemed amused.

"And now you and I can't never go steady, can we? And you were just getting to get so tall, too!"

He wanted to weep. He had not seen that he was getting taller.

"I could visit."

"You won't."

"I could write."

"But I'll be going with somebody else by then. Don't you think?"

"Yeah, but . . ."

"But we won't forget you, Lee. None of us will."

"*They* will," he said, nodding to the others who, some of them, appeared to have forgotten already.

It had begun to rain, but not so precipitously as to drive the people into the building itself. Moving on to Steve, Lee stood next to him for a moment, adding: "We're moving, my parents and me."

"Did you listen to *Jack Armstrong* yesterday? I didn't get to."

"Yeah."

"What happened?"

He explained, Lee, in shortened form what had happened, and then passed on toward Smitty, whose strands of peroxided hair had begun to run down over his forehead owing to the drizzle.

"We're moving," he started to say before then changing his mind and continuing on toward the larch grove at the further end, where Mildred was standing in partial shelter under the leafless branches. He let a moment go by before explaining to her, "We're moving, my family and me."

"Oh? Then you'll have a chance to start over again.

Good."

"Yeah, but . . . !"

"I just hope they can teach you something, that's all I have to say."

He spent the morning playing two sets of Nine Men's Morris with Preston. Finally, with ten o'clock fast coming up, he arose from his place and, moving slowly backwards, let himself out into the corridor. Someone was smoking at the far end, but whether it were a student or a member of the faculty, he couldn't be certain. It appalled him that someone had tried to enhance the pornographic artwork in the boys' room, changing it from a more or less normal experience, he supposed, into a creature with adventitious arms and legs. This time they were throwing dice, the half-dozen seventh- and eighth-graders gathered there.

"Well," said Lee, yawning and putting on a blasé expression. "Looks like we're moving, my parents and me."

"That's right, we ain't good enough for you. Shit, I knew you'd be leaving, first time I saw you!"

"Naw, he's alright."

"I wouldn't say that."

"He's had more licks than you ever had!"

The boy rolled. Lee moved closer to read the yield, but wasn't able properly to interpret it.

"How many you had?"

"Well," said Lee. "I had twenty-five the first time."

"'First time?' How many times you had?"

Lee counted. It had taken this long to accrue the respect that he had earned.

"Well, shit, I'm sorry you're leaving."

"Me, too; I'm sorry, too," said the Navy veteran. "And boy howdy, the women sure do like you, too! Here, Sloan, take a look at this."

Lee accepted the device, a thing that looked like a telescope, only about two inches long. Bringing it up to his eye, he viewed something that he had never seen before, a fully undressed woman with her legs up in the air. He lauded it loudly and raved about it, but even so was a little bit disappointed that her pubis wasn't any more complicated than she was. Herebefore he had always construed the female orifice as like a camera shutter.

The afternoon was spent in the usual way, and by three o'clock the whole town knew his fate. Sitting in place with his instrument, he was given a reed by one of the other clarinetists, a piece of generosity that was followed by an invitation to a Saturday night dance being sponsored by a crowd of girls who, most of them, were already well-known to him. That dance and those girls, they supplied the material for the next and final chapter.

Fifteen

The last day of his life, he climbed the stairs and took his place among the dozen boys standing with their backs to the wall. It was dark enough and that, together with the Nat King Cole edition of "Mona Lisa," had already put him in his favorite frame of mind. It is true that his nerves were poor, whereas his headache, never entirely absent, had coagulated at the bottom of his mind where he could ignore it.

"You have to give them credit," he said to the pale individual standing next to him. "It *is* dark."

They looked at each other. This person was from another town or school, as Lee could see by looking at him. Even so, he offered to shake with him. Would they or not play "My Foolish Heart," as rendered in the molten voice of Billy Eckstine? He could not have counted the girls whom he would have enjoyed dancing with to that particular tune—nine of them at least. He looked to Sandra who, however, appeared to have gone blissfully to sleep on

Cecil's shoulder. Suddenly Lee jumped back, avoiding Naomi's inquiring glance.

She was in a green satin dress that, to be truthful about it, really did go rather well with the sort of person she was. Comparing and contrasting that girl and dress with those of Barbara, he was reminded of the sway that beauty and personality exercise over those as know how to appreciate such matters. Let him have Gwen's facial features, Barbara's figure, Mildred's grey cells, and Lizabeth's laughter (she hasn't been mentioned yet), and he might still have some happiness before too late. That was when "Ebb Tide" came on, a new interpretation sung in an accent. Those old Europeans! No one knew more about love than they.

"You going to dance? Or not?" (Smitty talking.)

"Sure!"

"When?"

"Well, what about you? When are *you* going to dance, for example?"

"Ain't nobody going to dance with me!"

That was true.

"Besides, this here is probably the last dance you'll ever have. Since you're leaving us, I mean."

He was dressed in a white shirt and tie, together with last year's dungarees. Looking into his face, Lee could see no future for this boy save perhaps as a grocery clerk or gasoline attendant. And yet, all in all, he would have preferred to associate with this one than with the greater part of the people in his own neighborhood.

"I'll get somebody to dance with you," Leland in his rash way then volunteered.

"Who? Hey, I don't want any of them real fat girls, okay?"

Lee agreed to it. Barbara was busy, and Gwen was, too; going therefore to Naomi he drew her aside. "Want to dance?"

"All right." (Her eyes sparkled.)

"But I'm worried about Smitty. Nobody *ever* dances with him."

Her eyes traveled over to Smitty, whom of all boys she most despised.

"Please, Lee."

"Think how it feels. He's never, never, never, ever danced with anybody at all."

Again, she looked in the boy's direction. She was softening, as Lee could plainly see.

"Oh, all right. But just one, okay?"

He sent her off with gratitude and then waited to see if the boy would accept her. Across the floor, a new girl had entered the scene, a tall sort of person with her hair made up to look like a movie actress. Had ever he seen this person before? Yes, he had seen her in the Canteen in the days before he had tired of that place. He knew this much, that she was a year or two older than himself and perhaps even more than that.

"I dare you," Steven said, who had come up out of nowhere.

"Who is she?"

"Doesn't matter who she is. Just look at her."

"Yeah, but how old is she?"

"It don't matter how old she is! Shit, you'll be that old, too, someday."

"Why don't *you* dance with her?"

"You kidding? I don't have that kind of nerve."

That did it—Lee had no choice now but to make a fool of himself.

"Okay, if I have to."

"Wait a minute, I want Steve to see this."

He hesitated, however. Suddenly he experienced, Lee, a hand upon his neck, and behind that hand, Cecil's hideous strength.

"I hope you don't think you're just going to stand around all night."

"No, no," said Lee.

"You ought to be dancing with Naomi."

"I would, but she's dancing with Smitty. Actually, I'm thinking about dancing with that . . ." he pointed to the tall girl ". . . tall girl."

"Zoë? Shit, boy, she'll eat you alive! I used to know somebody who went with her."

Lee could feel his headache.

"No, that's okay, go ahead and dance with her if you want to. You need the experience."

"I guess not."

"Do it."

"Naw."

"I'm getting mad at you. I can always tell."

Lee pushed off. The girl was standing in the relaxed and confident way that seemed to say she was older and more acquainted with things than people realized. Cecil was watching, as also Steve and half a dozen other people. Lee put on a bored face but then veered off at the last instant and went instead to collect a glass of the green punch with lemons and limes floating in it. The music was playing "Jezebel," a song uncannily representative of his own situation at that particular time. And if at first he had been taken aback by the saffron and lavender gown the girl was wearing, he reconciled himself to it. Those hues were unified, as it were, and brought together by her own living person. Lee went up to her: "Want to dance? Naw, you don't have to."

She laughed. "With you?"

"Yeah. Cecil is with Sandra."

She put down her punch—a good sign—and then towed him—she was strong—out to the middle of the floor. The music had changed over to "Long Ago and Far Away," a morose sort of song that immediately made him feel as if everything that he had done or ever would had also happened long ago and far away. And then, too, he knew that it was being bruited about by modern science that someday life itself must end. Thinking about that, he experienced a wish to put his own life into motion and score some achievements while he still could.

"You sure do dance good!" he said, looking up at her. Her clothes were as described, while the girl herself was as white as a marshmallow or interior of an apple, or new-painted house. Would they, or not, play "My Foolish Heart" while he had this one in his arms?

"Thank you," she said, referring back to what he had said about her dancing.

"No, it's okay. Anyway, it's true."

It was not especially true, and by this time he would actually have preferred to be with Gwen or someone like that. On the other hand, he was being observed by some four or five grinning friends who respected his nerve. Could anything be more dispiriting than that, to find that one's reputation was increasing at the very moment that same person was about to move away?

"We're leaving, my parents and me."

"I thought he was going with Gwen," she said, referencing Cecil.

"He used to."

"He likes blonde girls, right?" *Her* hair was black, but she tossed it anyway.

"Yeah. But he likes brunettes, too. He's my best friend, actually, one of 'em." The music had ended without Lee being acutely aware of it, and the next he knew, they were dancing to "Sin," a new song that contained some especially fine lines, it seemed to him:

Take away the breath of flowers,
it would surely be a sin.

Lee hadn't expected the girl would actually begin humming to it. Truth was, he liked her and that she was devoid of any very obvious inhibitions.

"You hum good, too."

She laughed.

"But I'll still be able to come back and visit sometime," Lee attested.

"He's the fastest runner in school, is what they tell me."

"Yeah."

They danced through that song and two others before she towed him back to the punch and fished out one of the limes and began sucking on it. He took that to mean, Lee, that his time was over.

"Well, thanks for dancing with me," he said.

"Sure, honey."

He bowed. His collar was too tight and he was not attuned to wearing a knotted tie. In point of darkness, the room was about as dim as ever he had seen it, and he must remember to congratulate the girls who had managed things in such a way. Darkness and girls, perfume and punch—he couldn't understand why all of life shouldn't be the same. Suddenly that moment he perceived Cherise (high heels, scarf, pink dress) standing alone at the edge of the floor. He raced to her, arriving before anyone else.

"Hi!" he said. "Want to dance?"

"Well. I guess."

She was no taller than he. Gathering her in, he was smitten by her perfume, a styptic smell, astringent to a degree, that went direct to the brain centers of his head. Gazing into her eyes with concentrated focus, he witnessed that her earrings had little blue stones in them that matched her eyes, done deliberately, he suspected. She was so clean and fresh, she took at least two baths a day, he guessed.

"We're moving, my parents and me."

"Well, that's no good. We can't have that, Lee."

He agreed.

"Have you talked to them?"

"Oh, I've talked to them, all right! Doesn't do any good."

"Well, maybe you can come visit sometime."

She danced well, a function of her quintessential nature. Another three years and she would have become so devastating he wouldn't have been able to bear it.

"In my opinion," he said, turning serious, "you're going to be the best-looking girl in Alabama, you and Barbara."

"I'm worried about Barbara, poor thing. Those little freckles."

They danced. Life was short, the girl was pretty, and he had only to jump up and down and turn around and she will have turned into a construct of bones—these were the sort of thoughts that interfered with his evenings. Standing eye to eye, he could see how her jaw ended in a hinge.

"They probably won't let me visit very much. Once a year, maybe. But that's about all."

"They won't be going together very long."

"Heck, no. Anyway, he's going with Sandra now."

"Look, he even wears those boots at parties!"

"Yeah. He bought 'em with his own money, too."

Her shoulder was of just the right kind, neither too thin nor the other way around. Suddenly he found these following words breaking free despite his efforts to slow them down: "Maybe *we* ought to be going together, you and me."

"No, you're going with Naomi."

Lee waved it off.

"Besides, I don't steal other girls' boyfriends. Like some people."

"Maybe he stole *her*."

"Ha! Why would anybody want *her*?"

"You can't ever tell."

They danced. He could have reminded her, had he so

wanted, that the music had ended. Women's flesh, he couldn't understand it. Porcelain and ambergris, as he mooted humorously to himself. Looking into her eyes, he could very well see the little rods and cones, blue and gold, going about their eternal readjustments.

"If I'm like this at eleven," he cautioned to himself, "what would I have been at eighteen?"

They continued for another few moments, but "My Foolish Heart" never returned. Finally, the girl pulled back and expressed her pleasure.

"Thanks, Lee; you're a real sweet boy."

"Yeah. Say, did you know I'm going to be thirteen in just a few months?"

"What happened to twelve?"

"That's what I meant—twelve."

"And someday you're going to find just the right girl! I'm sure of it."

"Doubt it. They don't have these kinds of girls where I'm going."

"That's sad. Now don't you forget to come visit us, you hear?"

"Be dead by then."

The level of the punch had been falling fast, and by the time he returned to the bowl, there remained only an inch or two of sediment and rinds. His friend Steven had meantime gotten bogged down with a red-headed girl from some other school, a wild-looking personality with flowers in her coiffeur. The place was quieter than usual, no doubt because of a Les Paul and Mary Ford song that had come on. The strange thought then came to Lee that perhaps the outside world had disappeared and none were left alive but these fifty people, smiling in the dark. Soon they would belong to the antique past, and these present-day people would look back upon them, if they did, with but a sort of bemused condescension—he had noted this modern proclivity. This brought him to the Babylonians, who had perhaps cherished *their* moments just as much as he his.

It was then that "My Foolish Heart" came on for only the second time, arriving not when he was in Barbara's arms, nor Gwen's, but when he had just stepped outside to see if the world still existed. There was no question but that this was his favorite piece and that if he had his way, he'd be dancing with both those girls at the same time, together with others as well. Listening to that voice, he put some slack in his tie (always too tight) and set off in search of free agents no one had claimed as yet. There were numerous of these, but authentically pretty ones were thin on the ground.

He found one, as he thought at first, till she came into better focus. In any case, his interest had come to roost upon a brown-headed girl in a brown silk dress (this, too, done deliberately) fitted out in a sash of some kind. Unlike the first girl, this one girl actually grew prettier as he came nearer, ending finishing up as a true beauty who bore comparison, if not with Barbara, with Sonya at any rate. He stopped. He had known this person, he was sure of it, having first acquainted himself with her in third grade.

"Hi!" he said. "You probably don't even remember who I am!"

He had stridden too far, clashing into her nose with his much larger one. He was nearsighted, of course, always had been.

"Hi," he reiterated. "I'm one of Cecil's friends."

"That's nice. Which one are you?"

He pointed to himself, saying, "Got fifty licks so far. Don't know about Cecil."

"Twenty. I heard you didn't have hardly any at all."

"Oh, for God's sakes. You would have to of been there! By the way, do you remember when we were in Mrs.

Thornberry's class? Boy!"

"I just moved here last summer."

Lee jumped back. All those memories, those photographs of the mind, they belonged to someone else.

"Want to dance?" he asked. It is true that his favorite song had ended, to be followed, however, by "I Can't Stop Loving You" that was almost as good. She danced well enough, and he let a full minute go by before he began questioning whether this one would be his wife. No, she lacked that deep and mellow quality that he demanded in wives of his.

"You sure do dance good," he claimed.

"Thank you."

"Pretty good. You going with anybody?"

"Maybe."

"Who is it?"

She nodded shyly in the direction of Preston, a former friend of Lee's who happened in actual fact to be going with Molly Parker.

"He's going with Molly."

"Oh. Well, what about that one, is he going with somebody?"

"Naw, that's just Craig. Myself, I'm not going with anybody either at this particular time."

"But you used to be going with somebody?"

Lee said nothing. They had drifted close to Cecil and Sandra, who had fallen asleep in one another's arms and become one person. Coming nearer, Lee looked into the lovely girl's face from just inches away, finding there the image of a serene lake with flamingo accessories and dark yellow Moon overhead. He would not have resisted, not at all, had Cecil wanted to trade partners with him. Truth was, he had been wrong, quite wrong to have imagined he could be satisfied with a second-tier girl.

He guided his partner back to whence he had taken and thanked her politely for the enjoyment of the dance.

Steven had drawn off into the cloak room meantime to finish the packed lunch his mother had prepared. The music had begun to repeat, and many of the more prudential people—Lee despised them—had abandoned the building to stronger hands. Cecil, taking intermission from the prettiest girl in Alabama, had gone to the punch bowl (empty now save for a few withered lemons and shards of ice) and was smoking a thin black *cigaretto* hidden in the palm of his hand. There was but one last chaperone in the place, a tired-looking woman who would have gone home by now, had she had her way. Lee trained his Will on her, causing her to look up briefly and scan the area.

"I've been dancing with Gwen quite a bit," confessed Lee to Cecil.

"I saw you. And what's Naomi been doing all this time?"

"I don't know. Something."

"Look, my boy, these people aren't going to fall in love with you just because you want 'em to. You got to *force* 'em."

"Force 'em."

"That's right. Just keep working at it, and pretty soon they give up. 'Course now, sometimes *you're* the one that gives up."

"And so you give up?"

"No, no! Shit, boy! Don't *never* give up, not ever."

Lee also noted this down in the notebook of his mind.

"Cecil?"

"Hm?"

"How many girls have you . . . ?"

"'Bout sixteen, more or less. 'Course now I'm not saying I kissed *all* of 'em."

"Some of 'em, but not all."

"Right."

"Whew!"

A strange boy just then came up, peered into the punch, and then slumped down hopelessly in the nearest chair.

"You leave this town, you won't never kiss anybody—that's my prediction."

"They got girls down there, too."

"Sure they do. But what kind of girls? Shit, they won't be *anything like* what we got here. Just look at 'em. Look."

Lee looked, his gaze running into Barbara and Gwen, Sonya and the others. He wanted to cry.

"And I'll tell you something else, too. You get down there and you'll start being a different kind of person."

"Not me."

"Bullshit. *College*—that's where you're headed."

Lee snorted and then set out patiently once again to explain about his short fate.

"And you'll be wearing a goddamn little suit every goddamn day of the week!"

The boy was getting mad. Lee coughed twice and then strove to change the conversation.

"I suppose you and Sandra'll be married, next time I see you."

"Doubt it. Hell, no. No, she's pretty much the same kind of person you are."

Lee jumped back.

"College, and all that shit."

"Well, maybe she'll marry *me*," Lee said humorously.

"Doubt it."

"I doubt it, too," the strange boy added.

"Anyway, you aren't never coming back here. Never, never, never."

"Sure! To visit."

"No, you won't."

"Hey! She's gone!"

It was true. Taking her umbrella and scarf, the chaperone had left the floor, and at this moment was hobbling down the rather steep staircase that led to the city. It had *not* disappeared, the world outside, but simply become extraneous. Seeing all this, Cecil excused himself and hurried off to Sandra, a choice that left the remaining girls (and there were several of them) for Leland's use alone.

It was past ten o'clock in the evening when the last of those girls departed, leaving nothing for either of them. He was to remember one girl in particular, her pink gown billowing up about her like a cloud of cotton candy as she clambered into her father's car.

"Sleep well!" said Lee, directing the words silently in her direction. "Presuming tonight's excitement subsides enough to let thee!" He turned then to Cecil and, speaking in real voice, offered to shake with him.

"Well. 'Bye."

"Bastard. You'll be sorry."

They shook anyway, and the last Lee saw of him, the boy was trundling off homeward to the tune of the little silver chains that adorned his boots.

The night was clear, and the people, insofar as there still were any, were carrying umbrellas. Lee perceived a double-deck airplane running through the bloated clouds. Life had just seven stages, and he had used up two of those already. He spun around and then ran forward for the space of about a block and a half. The night was cold, and the oxygen had a salubrious effect upon his lungs and outlook.

"Ah, me," he said. Soon he would have left the commercial district altogether and, moving with the night, would have reached the district where Steve and Mildred dwelled. He passed Lacy's place and then, in quick succession, six well-known houses (well-known to him), their chimneys all plugged with stork nests. It was seldom that his headache was as thin as now or as tenuous; one might almost say that he hadn't any. He stopped, tempted to go back for the screwdriver he had left behind. Naw, it was too late for that.

At that time there was a house that had a shed that opened on the alley. Lee had deliberately chosen to come home by way of that alley, knowing that it was marginally more dangerous than the usual way. (He had long ago promised never to avoid the risks that might be offered him over the course of his seven stages.) And then, too, the shed was less than a hundred yards from home.

Entering with trepidation, he felt his way until he could determine that it had no people in it. Reaching the back wall, he turned then and looked out upon the outside world, as if he were lodged in a camera and the open door, as it were, were a shutter with a rectangular opening. He could see a good deal, but no one could see *him*, a scheme that later on he was to adopt as the pattern of his life.

But not quite yet! Still full of music and girls, of America at its best, and all the places still to see . . . He was not unhappy. That's how it was that year.

ABOUT THE AUTHOR

Tito Perdue was born in 1938 in Chile, the son of an electrical engineer from Alabama. The family returned to Alabama in 1941, where Tito graduated from the Indian Springs School, a private academy near Birmingham, in 1956. He then attended Antioch College in Ohio for a year, before being expelled for cohabitating with a female student, Judy Clark. In 1957, they were married, and remain so today. He graduated from the University of Texas in 1961, and spent some time working in New York City, an experience which garnered him his life-long hatred of urban life. After holding positions at various university libraries, Tito has devoted himself full-time to writing since 1983.

He has published eighteen novels. His first novel, 1991's *Lee,* received favorable reviews in *The New York Times, The Los Angeles Reader,* and *The New England Review of Books.* In addition to the present volume, his novels include *The New Austerities* (1994), *Opportunities in Alabama Agriculture* (1994), *The Sweet-Scented Manuscript* (2004), *Fields of Asphodel* (2007), *The Node* (2011), *Morning Crafts* (2013), *Reuben* (2014), the *William's House* quartet (2016), *Cynosura* (2017), *Philip* (2017), *Though We Be Dead, Yet Our Day Will Come* (2018), *The Bent Pyramid* (2018), and *The Philatelist* (2018)—which have been praised in *Chronicles: A Magazine of American Culture, The Quarterly Review, The Occidental Observer,* and at *Counter-Currents.*

In 2015, he received the H. P. Lovecraft Prize for Literature.